THE GLOW STONE

a novel by **Ellen Dreyer**

PEACHTREE
ATLANTA

A Freestone Publication

Published by
PEACHTREE PUBLISHERS
1700 Chattahoochee Avenue
Atlanta, Georgia 30318-2112

www.peachtree-online.com

Text © 2006 by Ellen Dreyer

Cover design by Loraine M. Joyner
Book design by Melanie McMahon Ives

Jacket front cover photograph courtesy of the United States National Park Service, Carlsbad Caverns National Park, New Mexico; photo by Peter Jones. Jacket back cover photograph of Fairy Caves, Glenwood Caverns, Colorado, ©2006 by Patrick Walsh, Inquisilab Enterprises.

Manufactured in United States of America

10 9 8 7 6 5 4 3 2 1
First Edition

Library of Congress Cataloging-in-Publication Data

Dreyer, Ellen.
    The glow stone / by Ellen Dreyer. -- 1st ed.
        p. cm.
    Summary: Sixteen-year-old Phoebe cannot help but wonder if she will suffer chronic depression like her mother and her recently-deceased uncle, who shared her passion for rock-collecting, until the terrifying experience of being lost in a cave provides the answer.
    ISBN 1-56145-370-6
    [1. Self-realization--Fiction. 2. Depression, Mental--Fiction.
3. Caves--Fiction. 4. Rocks--Collection and preservation--Fiction.
5. Family life--New York--Fiction. 6. New York (State)--Fiction.]
I. Title.
PZ7.D78397Glo 2006
[Fic]--dc22

                                                            2005027634

I am grateful to the people whose input and encouragement helped me in writing this book: Lois Adams, Aaron Barstow, Alison Blank, Jessica Clerk, Harvey and Doris Dreyer, Nancy Gallt, Marcia Golub, Susan Harris and family, Megan Howard, Irene Kelly, Marcie Maynard and family, Cory Munson, Wendy Murray, Julia Noonan, Constance Norgren, Jonathan Okin, Stephanie St. Pierre, Harriet Sigerman, Mark Strong, Lisa Trusiani, Jane Vecchio, Kris Waldherr, and Nancy Workman.

Thanks to Dorset Colony House and the Virginia Center for the Creative Arts for allowing me the time and space to work on drafts, and to the cavers of the Metropolitan Grotto Club for introducing me to the world below.

Special thanks to my wonderful editor Lisa Mathews, and to the entire staff of Peachtree Publishers, for going on this adventure with me.

And with gratitude always to my husband Jim and our son Aaron—you are my treasures.

—E. D.

FORMATION

I died once.

It happened exactly one year ago, when I was fifteen, on Memorial Day weekend, 2004.

Now, like then, I descend the cellar stairs, into the darkness that contrasts so strongly with the sunlit kitchen. Now, like then, the moist, cool air given off by the foundation stones creeps up my legs as if I am entering another climate. On the last step I hesitate before I land on the cold concrete floor.

A few of Mom's dishrags hang like flags from the clothesline strung the length of the cellar. My eyes follow the rope to its end and dart back and forth, first left to my father's workbench, then right to the red door. I exhale, suddenly aware that I've been holding my breath.

Okay, I admit it. I'm relieved. Somehow I wasn't certain the door would still be there, that it hadn't vanished. So much of what happened back then was all jumbled up with images that existed only in the dark of my mind. But my desk, my rocks, are a solid reminder that the events really did happen—and that, if I wish, I can go back to where it all started.

The thought makes me shudder and almost sends me running back up the stairs into the sunlight. I resist the urge to flee this solitude, this darkness.

Through the door, in the old cellar garage that nobody used, was my refuge: the one place I could be alone, away from the still, brittle air in the rest of the house, away from the weather of Mom's moods. There I could breathe and feel the fullness of myself, and not be afraid. There I kept the collection of rocks I'd been gathering for years.

"Here," Bradford had said as he pushed the shoebox into my hands. "Take it."

Though he was only sixteen then, my uncle stood tall: six foot three, lanky as a weed bending over me.

"What?" I whispered, knowing even as I opened the lid. I gaped at the three rows of specimens, neatly lined up on their cotton batting.

"See this one, Phoebe?" he said. "It's calcite, a carbonate. Commonly known as dogtooth spar. It's got eight sides—just like your age. Did you know calcites make up four percent of the weight of the earth's crust?" I shook my head.

Carefully, Bradford lifted the translucent green specimen, revealing a sliver of cardboard with the name written on it, and placed it in my hand.

"It really does look like a dog's tooth," I told him.

Suddenly, Bradford grabbed the gift back and nicked it with his thumbnail, leaving a white mark on one of the surfaces. "Did you think this rock was too hard to scratch?" he asked.

I looked up into his gray-green eyes. They glistened like the mineral in his hand, radiating fire. At other times, they could be so dark and still.

My surprise must have been visible on my face, because my uncle laughed. "Don't worry," he said, rubbing the scratch off with a corner of his T-shirt. "Some rocks are softer than they seem. You need to test them, to see."

That was the beginning.

⚜️

Now I stop and face the door. Shivers play along my arms as I place my hand on the brass knob. I jiggle it just enough to see that it will open, that I could go in if I wanted.

Do I want to?

My treasure, my rocks. Cold, indifferent, beautiful.

A shelter. A tomb.

Maybe it is pointless to relive the pain. Maybe it is better to let sleeping rocks lie.

CONGLOMERATE

May, 2005

Walking around the basement slowly, past the silent appliances, I let the cool dim atmosphere work on me, as if it could transform the mix of memories into something solid and smooth.

I mine the dark for bright bits of truth.

After Bradford died, everything was confused. A cloud had settled over everything: a constant cloud that didn't budge, that didn't let anything within it move, either. It would have taken something extreme to blow it away.

Even before then, though, there had been clouds.

I was about twelve when I first started hanging out in the old garage. One snowy, bone-cold Sunday afternoon, Mom and I had been arguing about something, and my own room didn't feel like a far enough haven. The old garage came to mind as a hiding place. No one ever went down there.

I remember my heart racing as I turned the knob, the cold blast of air as I pushed the door away and shone my flashlight into the still, dim cavern. Shivering, I stumbled down three steps, onto the dirt floor. What if there were a bogeyman behind the stack of lumber on that far wall, a gremlin in the cluster of old bikes? I swept my flashlight across the wall to my right and the large, barnlike doors rattling in the wind. A thin layer of snow had blown in beneath them.

Then I saw the desk.

It stood off to the side, protected from the elements. It was enormous: one of those old roll-top desks with many small, narrow drawers and compartments above its wide writing surface and bigger drawers, four on each side, below. I poked around in the cubbies first, finding old dried-up pens, scraps of paper with notes in faded ink, and larger, folded-up paper squares marked Topographic Maps. There were funny things, too—a kazoo, a pair of fake glasses with a rubber nose attached, green plastic soldiers carrying bayonets.

I figured Mom had bought the desk at one of the estate sales she sometimes went to, and that she couldn't find a place to put it upstairs. Even so, it seemed strange to stumble upon it in the garage. It was as out of place there as an elephant.

Later that evening, much as I wanted to give Mom the silent treatment, I had to ask her about the desk.

"It's your Uncle Bradford's," she said. "He

brought it down from Grandma and Grandpa's last week. It's a very old desk. I think he got it at an auction. He was keeping it in the cottage, but there isn't any space there anymore, since they took in renters."

I nodded. Out behind my grandparents' house upstate was a two-room cottage, with hearts carved into its shutters. Bradford liked it, and he often slept there. When we visited, sometimes he'd take a box of Bisquick from Grandma's pantry and fix us pancakes, which we ate sitting on a ratty, moldy couch. It wasn't much to look at; still, I envied him his private paradise back in the fir trees. After he'd moved to Pennsylvania to go to college, my grandparents had had the cottage fixed up to rent out. But as I tried to picture it all cleaned up, with strangers living in it, I felt a stinging hurt in my chest.

"Bradford was here?" I asked my mother.

She reached out, her fingers almost brushing my hair. "He had a lecture to go to in the city. He couldn't wait till you got home from school."

"Oh." My hurt softened to disappointment. Bradford was always heading into the city for some science lecture or conference.

"Actually," Mom went on casually, "he thought you might want to have it."

It took a full moment for me to realize what she was saying. "The desk? Me?"

Mom gave me one of her rare smiles. "Yes, silly-bean. Who else?"

"But doesn't he want it back? I mean, does he just want me to keep it for him a while?"

Mom shrugged. "He didn't say he wanted it back."

"Well, I'll call to ask…and thank him." I started up the stairs.

"What are you going to do with it?"

"Oh, I'll figure something out," I said, my head singing with joy.

She must have known what I was thinking. The gift of rocks that Bradford had given me four years earlier had multiplied into many shoe boxes full of rocks. Now he had supplied me with a perfect place to put my collection.

Gradually, over the next few days, I brought them down to the old garage. With the help of a book called *Rocks and Minerals*, I sorted and labeled them, then arranged them according to type in the desk drawers, which I'd lined with rolls of soft white cotton.

Sometimes I took the rocks out of their drawers and tested them. I scratched and scraped and examined them under a small microscope, and wrote my findings in a spiral notebook, the way Bradford had taught me. And sometimes I went down to the old garage and did nothing, just sat on the steps and thought, staring into the dark at the now-familiar shapes.

I imagined myself a geologist, going to the ends of the earth to bring back new specimens. I imagined the amazing rocks I would unearth—ones that museums would clamor for. I even dreamed of finding a spectacular stone that would inspire my mother to create a world-famous work of art. Back then, she was still painting a lot. It seemed as if her paints and brushes and easel and rags were as important to her as my rocks were to me.

Actually, Mom helped me expand my collection. Once in a while she took my sister Al and me to the Museum of Natural History in New York. I used my allowance to buy rocks in the gift shop. Mostly, though, I hung out in the Hall of Gems and Minerals, a dimly lit room with cases of sleek quartz crystals, bubblelike hematites, iridescent opals, and other wonders. My favorite was an amethyst geode as tall as I was and much wider: It had been cracked open, and within, it exploded in jewel-like purple crystal points. I stared inside a long time and marveled at how an object so rough and plain on the outside could contain such beauty.

Another thing about rocks—they don't break easily. When I held them, I wanted to be like them—strong and steady, weathered, but not broken.

I had never known anything like that, before or since.

I also collected rocks by digging in the backyard, scouting along stream banks in the park, or exploring any patch of ground I came across on family trips. Mom and Dad rarely said anything about my growing collection or about the many hours I spent in the old garage. Neither did my sister, except to tell me that if I didn't watch out I might turn into a blind mole rat from spending so much time in "that pit."

Bradford, though, was always curious about the rocks. From the moment I had called to thank him for the desk and told him what I would use it for, he had seemed pleased.

"I hoped that's what you would do," he had said. And he'd told me the desk was mine for keeps.

"For your next birthday, I'm going to find you an amazing piece."

"But you've already given me so much. Those rocks, now the desk…"

"No problem." I could see him on the other end of the phone line, waving me off. Then, the next February when I turned thirteen, he gave me a chunk of biotite gneiss, a flecked stone that changed colors depending on the light.

I loved that word, *gneiss*. You say it "nice." Gneiss…flint…quartzite…mica.

The names of my rocks sounded like magic, like music.

Feldspar…granite…amethyst…gypsum.

I would whisper their names aloud in the cool damp.

Back then, I had no notion that that same music would lure me into a place from which I almost didn't return.

First Stratum

1

May, 2004

*S*pider—*desk*. The words in the middle of Mom's to-do list floated up at me through the afternoon haze. I stared at them, only half listening as she gave her instructions. My sister Al, holding a bucket filled with cleaning supplies, stood next to me in the middle of the kitchen floor. Mom leaned against the counter, her head bowed, her profile pale. I knew she was worried that we'd never finish in time.

She needn't have been. Al and I were used to cleaning when she wasn't up for it, and today—the day before Bradford's unveiling—we were going to give it our all. We would polish the wood tables so you could see yourself in them and wipe the guilty fingerprints off each appliance. We would take the covers off the living room couches and wash off all our human debris.

But the desk...

The words on the list had taken a moment to settle in, I guess because I hadn't thought about the desk in months, and I couldn't remember the last time I'd looked at my rocks. They had fallen by the wayside, like so many things in the past year.

"What's that supposed to mean, 'Spider—desk'?" I heard the edge in my voice, the rising pitch.

"Spider," Al whispered loudly, grabbing my elbow.

Now Mom lifted her head. "It's time to sell it," she said without hesitation.

I felt my jaw drop and my cheeks redden, but she didn't notice—her eyes never left her list. She certainly couldn't see the cold wave of shock that flooded through my chest at that moment. "Forget it," I told her.

Al shook my elbow. I glanced at her long enough to see her furrowed brow that almost perfectly matched Mom's. I stepped away.

"It's my desk, you know it is. Bradford gave it to me," I told Mom's bowed, crescent-moon profile, almost eclipsed by loose strands of silver-streaked auburn hair.

She didn't respond. But of course she knew. She herself had told me it was mine.

Finally, she lifted her gaze to meet mine. Her gray eyes, so much like her brother Bradford's, had that dull look they took on when she wasn't feeling well. "It will be better," she said, more firmly, "not to live so close to the memories."

"Memories?" I repeated, as if it were a foreign word that I was just testing on my tongue.

"Yes." She attempted a smile. "Sometimes it's better to let go of things that remind us…" Her voice trailed off, and she dropped her eyes again. "So I think you should clean it out. Get it ready."

I willed her to look at me, to turn from her list and *see* me. It wasn't just the desk, it was the rocks inside it. All of what Bradford had given me, and all that I had made of it.

"I don't get it," I said. "Why would selling the desk make me feel better?"

Mom shook her head very slightly back and forth. She was remote again, unreachable.

Al yanked me toward the door. "Okay, Spide. Let's go."

"Wait," Mom said. She pointed to a small white candle in a clear holder, perched on the windowsill. A label pasted to the side of the glass read "Memorial Light." The wick was black, as if it had been lit and blown out. "We'll light the yahrzeit candle together."

I'd seen those candles before. Mom lit them for Grandma and Grandpa Bernstein the night before the anniversary of their deaths, and for a couple of other relatives who I didn't know.

"We don't follow many Jewish traditions, girls," Mom went on, "but this is one I feel is important. As a way of remembering."

Oh, I thought. *So it's okay to remember with a candle, but not with a desk, with rocks?*

I couldn't say it. All my muscles, including the ones around my voice box, had tightened up.

Mom reached into one of her shopping bags and pulled out an identical candle to the one on the sill—except that the wick was white, untouched. "I lit that other one earlier," Mom said, "but it kept going out. Something must be wrong with the wick—these candles are supposed to burn for twenty-four hours." Now she dug in her skirt pocket and pulled out a matchbook. She tore off a match. "So let's light this one," she said, finally turning to us. "I don't want to wait till sundown." She looked back and forth, between Al and me, deciding, and finally pushed the match and matchbook into my hand.

"No way!" I yelled. "Light it yourself!" I let the matchbook drop to the floor.

Mom listed to one side and Al caught her. I heard Al mutter "Oh, Spider," but instead of bending down to pick up the matchbook, I bolted out of the kitchen and through the front door, past Mom's car parked in the driveway, and into the street. I ran until my knees felt wobbly and my throat ached from breathing so hard. At last I stopped at the edge of the corner park.

The kiddie swings were going back and forth. "Higher, higher!" a little boy squealed. I sat down on the grass, sweating and breathing hard, watching the kids play. I kept going over what had happened in my mind, without making sense of any of it. Selling the desk...lighting a new candle to replace a defective one. Neither was a big deal, right?

Then I thought of Bradford. He was like that defective candle—he didn't make it to twenty-four, either.

I pressed my forehead against my arms and shut my eyes, trying to conjure him up as I often did, to bring him back. I hadn't seen him after he got sick, and his death had come so suddenly. Grandma and Grandpa Wiley had decided not to have a funeral, or to sit shivah, the seven-day mourning period after a death. I never understood it, any of it.

Opening my eyes, I lifted my head slowly, my hurt heart conjuring what I knew wouldn't be there: Bradford, alive, whole. Still, I sat, knowing I should move somewhere, anywhere.

Gradually the park emptied. A slight evening breeze blew against the swings, causing them to sway listlessly, chains creaking faintly. I watched the streetlights come on, and felt like the only person left in the world. When the feeling was too much to bear, I got up and went home.

❧

I followed the sound of sloshing water upstairs and looked in the bathroom doorway. Al stood in the tub, her back to me, swishing a scrub brush over the green tiled wall, her mouth stretched in a mildew-busting grimace. She had changed into a pair of cut-offs and one of her handmade tank tops, a sheer, purple paisley fabric that clung humidly to her curves.

"Hey," I said.

She stiffened, but didn't turn around. I grabbed a new sponge and a spray bottle from the bucket and headed for the sink area, which clearly needed attention. My face in the medicine cabinet mirror appeared cool and distant, like a moonstone. I quickly looked away. We scrubbed and rinsed for a few minutes without talking, which was fine with me. The steam from the hot water made it hard to breathe in the cramped bathroom, let alone carry on a conversation.

Finally she broke the silence. "You could have just lit the candle, Spide." Her tone was more weary than accusatory.

"So could you."

"I *did*." She slapped her sponge angrily on the wall. "After I led Mom to a chair and sat her down."

I turned to see her staring at the dripping, gleaming tiles, and I heard her sigh. Then I pressed my wet, sudsy sponge to the mirror, blotting out my blurred reflection.

"She wanted you to do it, not me," my sister said. *"Why?"*

"Because..."

We both turned at the same time and locked eyes. "She thought it would be good for you," she said.

I felt as bristly as a scrub brush just then. "How does she know what's good for me? Or you, for that matter?"

Al stepped out of the tub. "That candle—the flame, you know—symbolizes a person's spirit. So lighting the candle is a way of honoring his spirit."

"It's *her* way," I said, trying to hold down my anger. As I squeezed out my sponge, I saw my mouth in the clearing mirror, twisting downward.

"It's the *Jewish* way," Al said.

"We aren't even religious!" Despite my effort to stay calm, I felt my voice rising again. "Where are all these traditions coming from, all of a sudden? We didn't even have a funeral for Bradford!"

She held up her sponge and spray bottle as if she were about to throw them at me. Instead, she dropped them noisily into the bucket. "Just shut up, will you? Please?" She rubbed her hands against her thighs, drying them on her shorts. There was a kind of watchful desperation in her eyes. "God, I don't think I can get through this weekend—and I've got the cramps from hell on top of everything." She sat down on the rim of the tub, crossed her ankle over the opposite knee, and began massaging her Achilles tendon.

Al always got bad cramps when her period started,

and this was one of her natural remedies. Though she liked to remind me that I couldn't know how cramps felt—after all, I was the freak fifteen-year-old girl who hadn't gotten my period yet—right now, she said nothing, just massaged and sighed.

I sat down next to her.

"Listen, Spider," she finally said, "whatever it takes to get through this, okay? If it means lighting some little candle, just deal with it."

The two of us were silent a few moments. Then she went on, "You can see why I'm around here as little as possible. I don't know how I would've gotten through the past year if it weren't for Cam and Gretchen."

I nodded. Cam was Al's boyfriend, and Gretchen her best friend since third grade.

"See, you've got to get away, be around other people. And you need something else to do. That's why I spend so much time on my clothing designs and student government."

Much as I hated Al lecturing me, she and I rarely talked, and so I stayed put. Not to mention the fact that I didn't know where else to go. "I have friends," I told her. "Interests."

"Like who? What?"

I was mute. The fact was, I'd done my best to avoid other kids most of the school year, and even former friends had written me off. As for interests— well, I had my rocks.

"You can't be alone all the time. Call someone from school. Or—"

"Or what?" I felt my defenses rising up. My sister was sounding too much like my dad.

"Or maybe you should see that counselor, Mr. Ross."

I snorted. "Not that again." I'd seen Mr. Ross, the high school psychologist, two or three times after Bradford died last year.

"Well, it might help you...get over this." Al's voice rose up and down, like a lasso dropping on its target.

I sat there, very straight, very still. Why didn't anyone understand that I might not want to "get over" anything?

"The only part of me that needs help right now is my poor, numb butt," I said, rising from the tub rim.

She laughed weakly and slapped the back of my calf as we shifted positions. She took the toilet seat, and I sat cross-legged on the rug. "I don't know what we're doing in here," she said. "We should be starting on the living room."

"It must be ninety degrees in here."

"Easily."

We sat there a little longer.

"Sometimes I wonder," she said, "if she'll ever get over it."

"Mom?"

She nodded. "I mean, he was her baby brother."

I heard the faucet dripping, each hollow *plonk* marking time. *He was my uncle,* I thought. *My friend.*

"I miss him." I swallowed the sob that rose in my throat.

"Well, I miss...funny Brad," Al said. "You know the way he'd flap around, doing those bird imitations?" She smiled faintly.

I laughed. "Yeah. He was pretty good." In my head, I could hear his eagle shrieks resounding through the house.

"But sometimes it was hard to tell if he was going to keep it together..."

"You mean, not get too hyper?" I said.

"Yeah. Or that other extreme."

"Dr. Gloom."

Bradford was anything but even-keeled. He could be really agitated, in your face, so talkative you couldn't get a word in edgewise. Other times he'd lock himself in his room for hours on end, sometimes for a whole day. When he lived with us during the fall of his senior year while he attended a special college program in the city, we saw both extremes. But it was the middle ground I remembered best. During those calm times, he'd hang out with me, looking at rocks and talking.

Even then Dr. Gloom would sometimes appear and push me away. I could still feel the sting of hearing him say, "Go away, Phoebe," in a small voice that almost didn't sound like his own. My uncle always called me by my real name. In a family of nick-names—I'm Spider, for my long limbs, and Al's real name is Annelise—Bradford never used them. He said that a name expressed a person's essence, and that nicknames took away from that essence. I guess that was why he never wanted anyone to call him Brad.

"Anyway," Al said, snapping me back to the present, "I think Mom's right...about the desk. You should clean it out so she can sell it. I'm sure she'll give you the money, and then you can buy more rocks."

Sure. And where would I keep them? I avoided my sister's eyes, hearing it all in her voice. The boss, always insisting on the final word. She stood and stretched, picked up her bucket, and left.

Slowly I rose from the rug. I tore off a clean paper towel and finished scrubbing the toothpaste scum out of the toothbrush holder slots. Then, as I wiped another towel over the mirror, the clean glass cap-tured a sudden ray of sunlight, like a flame burning on the surface. I thought about the candle, about run-ning out on Mom. A sharp pang caught me in the ribs, near my heart.

2

I scrubbed the toilet, then rinsed out all my cleaning tools and left the bathroom. At the top of the stairs I heard Al talking on the phone in the downstairs den. Her voice sounded oddly cheerful, as if it belonged to some other girl in some other house.

I knew I should hurry—Mom would be home soon—but instead I lingered, looking at the pale rectangular patches on the stairway wall where Mom's paintings used to hang. She took them down a few months after Bradford died, around the time she stopped painting. She said that she'd lost the desire, that she no longer saw the point, and that she didn't want to look at such amateurish work.

I remembered watching her pack away her paints and brushes. I was amazed how carefully she handled them, even at the moment when she was giving them up. I didn't know what to say to her as she closed the box and carried it to the attic, as if the box were a tomb and she were burying a part of herself in it. In my mute shock, I also saw the sense of it, in a way: after what had happened, how could any of us be ourselves again?

When I reached the bottom of the stairs, my eyes were drawn to the photographs crowding the living room mantle. A couple of the pictures were of Bradford. In one he was a little boy, holding a teddy bear on his lap. In another he was around my age, lanky, with straight brown hair and soft gray eyes, half-hiding behind a tree with his arm around it and his cheek pressed against the trunk. He was good-looking, with those big Wiley eyes and high cheekbones, though he didn't seem to know it. In fact, I had the feeling the person taking the picture had had to persuade him not to disappear all the way behind that tree.

"Hi, Doctor Gloom," I whispered, rearranging the pictures so that his could be out in front.

There was another picture, hidden by the others, of a teenage boy sitting on a stone wall, his legs dangling to the ground. If you didn't know better, you'd think it was Bradford. But this boy's nose was straighter than Bradford's, and he wore his hair in a crew cut. It was one of Mom's cousins—Eric? Eddie? I'd never met him.

My eyes shifted back to Bradford. "We're going to the cemetery tomorrow," I told him. "We're going to see your grave."

He peered out at me like some kind of curious forest sprite, wild, unused to human contact. In my mind's eye I saw another image: Bradford, older, shivering in the cold rain. His tent had blown down, and he and the other campers struggled to find some kind of shelter.

That much I could picture. My uncle was strong and agile, and he wasn't afraid of the outdoors. What I couldn't see—the rest of it—was Bradford lying motionless in a hospital bed, dying from a heart attack brought on by his pneumonia-weakened lungs. The others had gotten him to the hospital as quickly as possible, but it was too late.

That's what they had told Al and me. Yet whenever I thought about it, like now, a knot of anger welled up in my throat. I turned from the pictures and went to the kitchen doorway. The candles sat on the windowsill: The defective one was cold, extinguished. The other's tiny flame was reflected in the darkening glass.

Bradford had had plans. He'd wanted to be a botanist, to study plants in the Amazon when he was done with college. Just because it was taking him longer than usual to finish didn't mean he wouldn't.

I stared at the candles, remembering, with a growing sense of disbelief. How could Bradford have had a weak heart and not known it? And why was Mom so determined to sell that desk, the one that belonged to me, the one that Bradford loved?

I went through the kitchen, to the top of the basement stairs, and took the first step downward. Anger throbbed so hard in my throat that I almost couldn't swallow. I'd been over the story, again and again, with Mom and Al and Dad, and it never made sense. Still, for lack of any other explanation, I'd begun to believe it. Or maybe I was simply sick of *not* believing.

The next thing I knew, I was standing before the red door, my hand on the knob. I turned it until I heard a click and let myself in.

Right away, I saw that someone had been there. The utility lamp lay on the floor beside the desk, its bulb missing. As I panned my flashlight across the desk, I noticed that some of the drawers had been left open. My hands shook as I pulled the drawers out all the way, revealing the specimens inside, laid out so carefully on their cotton batting. Nothing had been changed or moved. Looking at the rocks, I felt the sharp edge of my anger dull.

Rocks always filled me with wonder.

The middle drawer held the metamorphics— rocks that began as igneous or sedimentary and were altered by heat or pressure into a different form. I stroked the smooth surface of my biotite gneiss, then my migmitite, a piece of schist with a snakey pattern of granite running through it.

In Greek, *meta* means "change" and *morph* means "form." Metamorphic—a useful word. It could probably describe my life right now.

I closed that drawer and opened one filled with miscellaneous specimens all jumbled in a pile. I'd never know if they'd been messed with. Still, I knew without a doubt that my mother had been here.

I replaced the lamp on its wall hook, and using my flashlight I browsed through the small upper drawers. These contained only a few specimens each. My best. Each one sat on the cotton batting with a sliver of an index card beneath it. On the sliver I'd written, in tiny letters, the name of the rock or mineral and where it had been found. *Feldspar— Labrador. Obsidian—Iceland. Biotite Gneiss—Montana.*

I picked up the gneiss before I noticed the crack down its middle. The two halves fell apart and lay there in my palm: two gray jagged surfaces flecked with crystal and lined with bands of pink granite. I closed my hand over them, as if I could weld the two pieces back together…as if I could make them whole. Of course, when I opened my hand, the pieces fell apart again, and the anger came back full force, pressing on my chest so I almost couldn't breathe. *Did she do this too?*

Then I saw the tiny white card that lay on the cotton batting.

"For Phoebe," it said, "my favorite rock scientist."

Uncle Bradford's gift.

Had Mom picked it up?

I set the card back on the cotton, put the two broken pieces of gneiss on top of it, and shut the drawer.

This wasn't just a desk. It was my place.

After double-checking that all the drawers were shut tight, I turned away and went back through the door, crossing the basement and climbing the stairs, into the light and heat of the kitchen. I saw Al through the doorway, kneeling on the living room carpet, attaching the hose to the vacuum. She didn't look at me or say a word as I approached.

I picked up a clean rag and started polishing the coffee table. My arm made rhythmic, familiar motions that were comforting in a way. I knew what I had to do. It was all on Mom's list: Make the surfaces spotless. Remove even the memory of dirt and dust.

3

After we finished the living room, a little before four o'clock, Al decided she needed a break and went to make another phone call. I told her I'd get started on the kitchen—but I didn't right away. I had no desire to be in the presence of the candles, or of my mother, who had gone out again but was sure to come home any moment.

I went upstairs and padded down the hall to the doorway of my parents' room. The bed was unmade, the sheets in tangles. Mom's desk stood in a far corner, cluttered with books, and her dusty, folded-up easel leaned on the wall beside it. Clothes littered the floor. Normally, Mom didn't leave clothes on the floor, or didn't used to, anyway. Since Bradford's death, all that had changed.

There were boxes, too, packing cartons lined up under the windows, waiting. Was Mom planning to take more of her memories up to the attic?

"You can't get rid of everything," I said aloud, as

if she were standing there. As I spoke I saw the sunlight glinting off one of the books piled on the desk. I went toward it, curious to see what sort of antique Mom could be treating so carelessly.

As I got closer, I could see that there were tiny embossed gold flowers up and down the reddish brown leather spine. There was no title on the cover, just a border of the same flowers.

On another day, I would have left the book there—clearly it was something personal—but since Mom had invaded my privacy in the garage, I didn't know why I shouldn't take it out of the pile and open it. I even got a little jolt of satisfaction when I turned to the first page:

December 1979
My descent

The slanted cursive, written in ink the color of blue denim, was neater than Mom's—but it was definitely hers. "Oh, please. How pompous," I whispered, laughing a little under my breath. But a chill simultaneously ran down my spine. Descent? What was that supposed to mean?

I snapped the cover shut, telling myself I would just put the diary back in its pile, and Mom would never know the difference. Instead, I remade the stack without the diary, which I stuck up under my tank top. I hurried to my room, closing the door behind me, and sat on the end of the bed. Then I thought better of it and got up again to lock the door.

My room used to be the guest room. Bradford stayed here when he lived with us. He'd left behind his collection of sci-fi novels on the bookshelf, and a tiny drawing of a naked girl underneath a torn flap of wallpaper beside the bed. The wallpaper was a dark hunter green, many shades darker than the leaves of the maple outside the window. If it was up to me, I'd get rid of the wallpaper and paint the room obsidian blue.

I pulled the book out from under my shirt. It felt hot in my sweaty palms.

Put it back, said the good little voice in my head...the voice that was fading fast.

I opened to the first page again, and then I noticed lines scrawled across the bottom:

> *A bite of apple turns to ash,*
> *the wind whips heavy as a lash.*
> *The day's beauty crumbles away,*
> *revealing its true color, gray.*
> *Forgive me if I cannot stay.*

Outside, a car door slammed, and I jumped up. My hand trembled as I slipped the diary back underneath my shirt, while Mom's ominous little poem seeped into my brain. I knew I had to hurry if I wanted to return the diary to its stack on Mom's desk. But I only made it halfway to my door before something stopped me, and instead I lifted up my mattress and placed the red leather diary gently on the box spring.

As I lowered the mattress, I noticed that a trace of the red dye had come off on my hand. Wild drumbeats pounded in my head. I went to the bathroom and scrubbed my hand and stomach with a washcloth.

From the hallway I could see Mom at the bottom of the stairs, holding onto the banister with one hand and rubbing her forehead with the other. "Spider," she called, "would you unpack the groceries, please? I've got to lie down."

"Sure," I said.

But as she pulled herself up the stairs with the last bits of her energy, I wanted to shout, "Snap out of it!"

Then, as she passed me, I wanted to touch her shoulder, to apologize for running out on her earlier, to confess my theft—anything that would draw her pretty eyes out of their shadows. Instead I folded my arms and backed up against the wall to let her pass, waiting until she turned right and disappeared into her room.

Back down in the kitchen, I avoided looking at the tiny flame and got to work unpacking the eight bags of groceries—everything we would need for our weekend upstate, from cold cuts to veggie burgers, fruit to cookies. It seemed almost silly to have to put things away only to repack them tomorrow morning, but Mom never liked shopping near Grandma and Grandpa's house; she thought the grocery stores up there were too expensive.

As I worked, I thought about the diary. *My descent.* It could have meant anything, but together with the poem, it seemed to say that something really was wrong back then, when Mom was my age. And though the idea of reading on frightened me, I knew I would at the first chance I got.

When I finished putting away the groceries, I slipped on some rubber gloves and started scrubbing the countertops with a pine-scented cleaner. I was almost high from the fumes when Dad walked in at seven-fifteen.

"My industrious girl!" he bellowed. Startled, I looked up from polishing the kitchen table and smiled. Dad is a public relations man, and sometimes he comes out with phrases that sound like headlines.

I hugged him, smelling sweat and day-old after-shave. His beard, I noticed, had sprouted a new crop of gray hairs. "So?" he said, already turning to the mail, which lay in a wooden box on the counter. "How did your day go?" He thumbed through the letters while I finished the table.

"Okay."

He glanced at a couple of envelopes, then dropped the mail back in the box. "Really?" He yanked off his already loosened tie and draped it over his shoulder.

I wanted to rinse my scrubbing cloth and get back upstairs to the diary, but the next moment Dad was beside me, leaning against the countertop, his belly bulging over his belt a little more than it used to. Dad is a burly guy, and it is hard to ignore a burly Bernstein. He was staring through the window, or maybe at the reflection of the flame, brighter now that the daylight was waning. "Mom upstairs?"

I nodded.

"What did you do today?"

"Oh, you know. Cleaned."

He shifted, leaning into his side instead of his belly. "That's it?"

I swallowed. "No. I...took a walk."

"Ah. Good." He exhaled.

Telling lies, even white lies, wasn't something that came naturally to me. But I figured Dad wouldn't appreciate hearing I'd run out on Mom.

"Hey," he said, cupping his hand at the back of my head so I'd look at him. He seemed about to say something, but then he released my neck and ruffled my hair, just like he used to when I was little.

"Spider, are you okay, about tomorrow? About going to the unveiling?"

I jerked away from him. "What do you mean?"

He coughed nervously. "Nothing. But if it seems like too much—"

"Dad, unlike some people around here, I'm not made of glass." The irritation in my voice was barely checked.

His brown eyes seemed hurt and small, almost hidden in their shadowed sockets.

"I'm sorry," I whispered.

"No, *I'm* sorry, honey. I know you can handle it. It's important that we have a time to remember Bradford...together. And things will get better, afterward."

I nodded, wanting to believe it, the simple formula that Dad undoubtedly used to get through life: Things will get better. What kind of magic could possibly happen at the unveiling of Bradford's tombstone? But I didn't push my luck. I could see how tired Dad was, how little he wanted to talk about this.

"Did Aunt Erica call?" he asked, changing the subject. "She's driving down from Providence tonight. She probably won't make it for dinner, but we'll save her something. Does pizza sound okay? I'll go put some shorts on, then I'll come back down and order."

"Okay," I told him.

He lumbered out of the kitchen like a big bear, then headed up the stairs, his footsteps slow and heavy. I wondered if he would manage to coax Mom out of bed. Or maybe he'd just let her sleep through dinner.

I was glad Aunt Erica would be here soon. There's hope, I reminded myself. Having my favorite aunt around always lightened things, even in the worst of circumstances.

Breathe, I told myself, pushing through the kitchen door onto the deck. The air was slightly less hot and muggy than earlier in the day—and the near-twilight quiet was broken only by the cicadas' shrill song.

I looked out over the neatly manicured green lawn, and my eyes were drawn to a bush at the side of the house, all dry and scrawny-looking from the heat. When I was little, it had always seemed so big and lush, especially when I'd lie underneath it and gaze up at the sunlight coming through the leafy branches. But it wasn't the bush that had attracted me, it was the sparkling ground underneath it. I'd spent a lot of time on my hands and knees, digging in the earth for the chunks of gold. Later, much later, I found out that my treasure was really pyrite—fool's gold—but at the time, it looked real enough to me. Mom got sick of emptying my pockets of the stuff, and told me to find less messy rocks to collect.

"Spider." The wispy voice pulled me out of my reverie. I swung around.

There she stood, just inside the kitchen. Through the screen, she seemed indistinct, not quite solid. Her light blue sundress billowed around her bony frame. "Come here," she said.

I pushed through the door, into the kitchen.

"Did you do it, honey?"

My face flushed. Did she mean the diary? Did she know I took it? "What?" I mumbled.

"Clean out the desk."

"Mom—"

I heard Dad's footsteps, and then he appeared at the other end of the kitchen. Mom backed away, gravitating toward him; he rested his hands on her shoulders.

"I'd really like you to get to it," she went on.

"Mom, I'm *exhausted*. I've been working all day."

"I thought I'd put an ad in the paper this weekend," she went on, seemingly oblivious to my protests. "There are lots of tag sales over Memorial Day weekend."

"But we're going away," I said.

"Just for tomorrow. We'll be home on Saturday."

I sighed. "I thought we were spending the weekend with Grandma and Grandpa."

"No," she said.

"But I *want* to."

"We'll have a little time together…after…" Mom shook her head, her mouth set in a line.

I knew she meant the unveiling, but couldn't bring herself to say it.

Just then, Al walked in from the dining room. "I'm going out with Cam," she announced, then realized she'd entered a hornet's nest. She dropped her sing-songy tone. "What's up?"

"Maybe," Mom said to me, "Al could help you. If you both start after dinner, you can get it done."

"Mom, I just told you I'm going out," Al repeated,

sounding a little frantic. "Cam's coming to pick me up."

"That's fine by me," I told Al, my voice heavy with anger.

"Cam will have to wait, Al," Mom said, ignoring me. "You can put it off to another night."

For a moment, I thought my sister might cry, but all she did was sigh dramatically.

"Al," Dad said, "why don't you order the pizzas? You can pick whatever you like on them."

Al lingered there, eyeing Mom, as if that would make her change her mind. We were like some chess game in progress, facing off, each on our tile squares. Someone had to move, to break the charged tension.

"Mom," I said, almost shouting. "Why did you go down there? Why did you break my rock?"

She brought her hands to her face, covering her eyes.

"You know that desk is mine," I went on. "Bradford gave it to me." I heard the anger in my voice, and the strength. "So you can't decide whether to sell it or not. That's my decision."

A cry broke out of Mom's throat. "It's not good for you to hang around so much in that dark garage!" The high-pitched words burbled out. Then, as if her words had unleashed a dam, she sat on the floor and wept.

"Baby," Dad said, rushing forward, scooping her up under the arms.

I stared at them, cold anger morphing slowly into panic.

"Come on, now," he soothed, and she found her footing again, leaning her head on his shoulder. "Come up and rest."

When they were gone, Al looked at me in disbelief. "Man, you're batting a thousand today," she hissed, as their footsteps ascended the stairs.

"All I said was the truth!"

"Truth, schmooth. You could have just gone along with her. Geez, Spide, that isn't the only old desk in the world, is it?"

"Thanks, sis, for all your support."

She let out another exasperated sigh, stalked over to the wall phone, and picked up the receiver. "So what do you want? Onions? Green peppers?"

4

Hi there." Aunt Erica stood in the porch light, all four-foot-ten of her, smiling, her long black hair clipped to the top of her head. She looked younger than thirty-four in her red overalls and white T-shirt, and I realized I was at least a head taller than her. She noticed, too: her eyebrows went up and she nodded as if impressed. Then she reached out and gripped me in a hug that reminded me of her true strength.

I could have stayed there a long time, but I felt like I was going to start bawling. I quickly pulled away.

"Did I crush you?" she asked.

At that moment, Aunt Erica appeared the way I always thought of her, smiling her wide, toothy smile that reminded me so much of Uncle Bradford's, her blue-green eyes flecked with yellow spots of light. She stepped back and took a look at me. "Phoebe Bernstein. It is good to set eyes on you."

Like Bradford, she always called me by my real name, not Spider.

"Thanks," I said. "Ditto."

She stepped around me and swung her duffel bag to the floor just as Al opened her arms for a hug.

"Hello, Annelise. It's good to see you too." She wrapped Al in her boa constrictor grip for a few seconds, then released her. "Mmm…" she said, wrinkling her nose. "I smell pizza."

"You came just in time for dinner," Al told her. "Lucky you. I ordered an extra one."

"Great," she said, kicking off her sandals. "I could eat a whole one by myself." There were footsteps on the stairs. We all turned to see Mom, followed close behind by Dad. I drew back into the shadow under the staircase.

"Aren't you sneaky," Mom said, giving Aunt Erica a kiss. "I didn't hear you coming up the path."

"Bet you didn't know I used to burgle during school vacations," Aunt Erica told her with a laugh.

"Just as long as you don't steal anything of mine," Mom shot back. It was such a strange thing to say, I turned to look at her. She gave Aunt Erica a little punch in the arm.

"Are you talking about your pizzas or your kids?" Aunt Erica joked. "I'll take one of each." She reached into the shadows and pulled me out.

"We'll make an exchange," Dad said. "A pizza for a blueberry pie." He scrunched his eyebrows pleadingly. "You did bring pie, didn't you?"

"Don't I always?" Erica said, looking around at

each of us as if we were shipwrecked and she'd come to our rescue. "I'll go bring them from the car." Her eyes, patient and sad, fell on Mom. "I think we could all use a little sweetness."

⁂

"So when do we leave tomorrow?" Aunt Erica said after dinner, as we sat around the table strewn with empty pizza boxes and blueberry-stained plates.

"Nine, ten at the latest," Dad answered. "That will give us plenty of time to get up there and have an hour with Sophie and Ben...beforehand."

Mom rattled the ice in her glass. "I told Mom and Dad we're not staying," she told Aunt Erica. "We're coming back tomorrow night."

Aunt Erica looked confused. "I don't understand. They're expecting us to stay over at least one night."

"Well, you can if you want to."

Aunt Erica made a little grunting noise in her throat. Her brow was scrunched up.

"I don't want to come home tomorrow." The words came out of my mouth effortlessly. "I want to stay."

Mom's eyes rested on me. "Sure. Just as long as you do what I asked you to do."

"*Fine,*" I said, pushing away from the table.

"Do what?" Aunt Erica asked as I headed for the basement steps. I heard Al starting to explain, but by then I was too far away to make out the words.

I grabbed some plastic shopping bags from a shelf

in the laundry room. I was glad for an excuse to get out of that kitchen, to be by myself for a little while.

Opening the red door, I went down the three steps, turned right, and reached for the rounded corner of the desk. The wood felt cool and smooth, like an ocean pebble. I kept my hand on it until my eyes had adjusted enough to see my pale skin against the old wood.

Yes, Mother, I will clean out the desk. The question is, where to start? And where will I take the rocks?

I switched on the weak overhead light and opened the top drawer of the desk. My crystals. No, I wasn't ready to tackle those. They were too pristine, too beautiful on their cotton bedding, with the tiny ID cards beneath them. Instead, I went for something easy: the lower drawer that contained large miscellaneous rocks. I pulled the drawer out until it tipped almost to the ground and picked up what looked like a conglomerate rock studded with pebbles and bits of flint. Kneeling, I shone my flashlight on it. The flint was shiny blue and gray as if it had been rolled on the ocean floor, and specks of rust clung to the holes where some of the bits had fallen out.

Mom wanted me to clean out the desk—and quickly—but I knew I could go only so fast with rocks. I'd never get this job done in one night. I opened two of the shopping bags and placed them on the desk. I would put the rocks I wanted to keep in one and the duplicates or the less-interesting rocks in the other. I examined each rock carefully before making my decision. After what seemed like a geo-logic age, I noticed that the keepers far outnumbered the discards. I sighed. Maybe I should take them all up to the closet in my room and find a better place to stash them later.

I reached for the bags, hesitated, then went back to the drawer that held my biotite gneiss. I took out the two halves and put them in my shorts pocket. Finally I lugged the bags up to the living room, past Aunt Erica, who was already asleep on the couch, and qui-etly climbed the stairs. Fortunately, all the doors along the hallway were closed and no one saw me slip into my bedroom. I dragged the plastic bags over to my closet and shoved them inside, amid the clutter of shoes and boots. *Let them rot there*, I thought, then realized how stupid that was: I would rot long before they did.

5

Some weekend mornings, as soon as we got up, Al and I used to make a beeline for Mom and Dad's room. We'd claim whatever spot could be found on their bed, amid the sections of newspaper, books, orphaned socks, and anything else that had gathered on it—not to mention our parents, pretending to sleep as we mock-fought, rolled, and curled up around them. Eventually Mom or Dad would say, "Weigh anchor, mates, we're setting sail!" and we'd take our posts on the port or starboard side. Then we'd vote on who the captain would be. The captain got to pick where we sailed to on our rumpled boat. I remembered holding on to the bedpost, eyes peeled for pirate ships, until someone mentioned breakfast.

It was a good memory, but it made me sad, and I clung to my bed like a life raft and listened to the waves of birdsong floating through the screened window. I didn't want to go back down to the old garage, even though I knew I should, and I certainly wasn't ready to face anyone. Judging by the silence inside the house, and the early hour—6:40 A.M.—no one was likely to be up yet anyway. I turned onto my side and pulled the purple sheet over my head. The moment I closed my eyes I remembered the diary, and I sat up so fast I was dizzy.

You don't take people's diaries, I told myself in a rush of guilt. *You don't steal their private thoughts.*

On the other hand, I countered, *you don't go into their private belongings, either. Not without asking.*

Trying to feel justified, I got up out of bed, lifted the mattress, and carefully pulled out the diary. From the corner of my eye, I noticed the streetlight going off outside my window. I locked the door and then sat down again on my bed. The worn leather book fell open to the first page.

December 1979
My descent

Again I wondered what she could have meant. It seemed creepy, and even the hurried slant of her letters made them look almost desperate, as if they were fleeing toward the edge of the page. I avoided the poem at the bottom and turned to the next page, where her name was written in a neater, more careful cursive:

Pamela Rachel Wiley

It floated there tentatively, fading into the soft-as-suede paper. Here I could see the familiar loops, the dash instead of a dot over the *i*. This looked more like Mom. I glanced away at the sun-dappled leaves outside my window. The day promised to be bright and scorching. But as I looked back at the diary, a pleasant, almost-cool breeze came through the screen and made the hairs on my arms stand up.

December 4
  I can't talk to anyone else, Grace. So it's going to be you.

Grace? She named her diary?

  I saw him, Grace. There, in the mirror. I know I wasn't supposed to look, but I did. I broke the law, and I'm going to regret it forever.

Reading her words, I felt as if I were swimming a long distance, winded and verging on exhaustion. My lungs constricted. There was a blank space in the middle of the page, and then, way at the bottom, some slanted lines of tight print:

  Grandma says the mirrors are covered so you don't look, because if you do, the Angel of Death will snatch away your soul, just like it did the departed's. But I didn't see any angel. I saw Eli.

Much as I wanted to pull away from the diary, I found myself turning the page.

December 30
Eli died on Christmas Day. I'm not going to tell you how it happened. I can't bear putting it on paper. I can't understand it. He was fine at Hanukkah when we were all together, telling stupid jokes that made everyone laugh. And now he's gone.

The funeral was two days ago. I'm not going to describe that, either. It was awful. Since then I haven't left the house. I'm afraid of what will happen if I show my face outside, how I'll react once I hit the air. How I'm ever going to survive going back to school, facing his friends, facing anyone...I don't know.

Eli. Mom's cousin. The one in the mantel photo, sitting on the brick wall. The one who looked so much like Bradford.

The next entry had no date:

I asked Mom about the mirrors. She said we cover them during the seven days we sit shivah so that we don't concentrate on appearances. It is a time to turn inward, to our hearts, to our memories of Eli.

She didn't say anything about the Angel of Death.

Mom's always saying Grandma's superstitious. Maybe that is just another one of her crazy ideas.

But what if Grandma's right? What if the angel that snatched Eli is trying to get me, too?

I quickly skimmed the next few entries, short passages about her first few days back at school. When I came to the middle of January, I started reading more carefully.

January 17
Dear Grace:

I'm sorry. Don't hate me. I just haven't been able to write lately. Eli's dead. Nothing's going to change that. What else is there to say?

Mom made me go talk to the school psychologist—what a joke. His eyes kept straying to the clock, and I saw him yawn a couple of times. I never realized I was so boring.

Then, idiot me, I came home and took a couple of Mom's pills. Well, more than a couple. I just wanted to go to sleep, to sleep forever. The next thing I knew I was waking up in the hospital. They'd pumped my stomach. I lay there for two days with a splitting, throbbing headache—which I deserved, I guess. The doctors thought I needed "observation"—as if my stupidity were some rare and fascinating thing. I wanted to tell them there's nothing to observe. I'm too stupid to even know how many pills to take. "It won't happen again," I kept telling everyone. "It won't happen again."

I closed the diary and placed it on my stomach, shifting my gaze out the window. Despite the bright sun, the leaves, unnaturally still, seemed duller than before.

Mom had tried to kill herself once. How could anyone be sure she wouldn't try again?

She was grieving then, and she is grieving now.

A metallic taste rose up from my throat; I thought I might vomit. I sat up and put my head between my legs, until the feeling started to pass. Then I got out of bed and moved around my room like a zombie, randomly picking up things—a vintage pen from the 1964 World's Fair that Dad had given me, a French quiz with a big red A- on it, a split amethyst geode— a miniature version of the one at the museum—that I used as a paperweight. It was reassuringly heavy in my hand, and the inside was encrusted with tiny purple crystal points.

Feeling better, I put the diary back under the mattress, where I hoped no one would think to look. Then I peeled off my sleep T-shirt and pulled on my favorite purple tank top and a fresh pair of jean shorts. I tiptoed downstairs to the hall closet, where I grabbed Dad's two gym bags. These would work better than plastic bags for carrying my rocks upstairs. I sneaked past the living room where Aunt Erica was still sprawled, and on toward the kitchen. I would do as much as I could in the time before we left, and then I could tell Mom that at least I'd made a start. I could tell her that I'd reconsidered, and she was right: it would be best to sell the desk.

Who cared that it wasn't the truth, if it would ease her mind a little.

My heart jumped when I saw Dad at the kitchen table, working behind the open lid of his briefcase, and I turned on my heels to get away before he heard me. Too late.

"Spider." He peeked around the lid. "You're an early riser this morning."

I hovered in the doorway, one foot in, the other out of the kitchen.

"Come here," he said, stretching his arms out. "Give your old dad a hug."

I wanted to run, but a sadness in his eyes kept me there. I let him give me a hug, then pulled away.

He started to tap the writing pad on the table with his pen tip. He nodded at the gym bags. "Whatcha up to?"

"Oh." I flushed. "I meant to ask…if I could use them for a while. To store my rocks, you know, till I can find another place for them."

"Sure." He smiled. "Keep them as long as you need to."

"Thanks." I was used to Dad siding with Mom— he and Al usually did—and for the first time, I was seeing the sense of it.

"Got any ideas for me?" he said.

I looked from his tapping pen to his eyes. "Ideas?"

"I need a slogan for Duncan Soups."

I shook my head again, half disbelieving. *How can you work now?* I thought. Still, I made the effort. "How about, 'Bad for the chicken, good for you?'"

He laughed. "If only I could be so honest."

"Daddy..."

The word slipped out so easily, even though I hadn't called him that in ages. He stopped his tapping, and his smile faded.

"Is Mom okay?"

He hesitated a moment. "You mean, after your argument yesterday?"

"Well yeah, but—" I took a deep breath, and then dropped my voice to a whisper. "Is she taking her medication? Does the doctor think it's helping?"

He set his pen down and folded his hands. "Sit down, sweetheart."

I slid into a chair, my heart pounding in my ears.

"You don't need to worry about it," he said. "The doctor thinks she's doing well on these pills."

"Is he sure?"

"Spider, honey..." His lips jerked ever so slightly, but he didn't quite manage to summon back a smile. "We've all had a hellish year, and you've got a right to be upset and angry. God knows, I've been." He stared out the window, as if to catch sight of the words he needed. "The unveiling will bring some closure for Mom, for all of us. I'm sure of it."

Bring closure. I couldn't help but hear his words

as tag lines, the phrases he wrote for ads to catch the reader's eye, to make him or her want to buy something. They didn't have to be absolutely truthful, just...persuasive. Still, he seemed to believe them. And maybe he was right—maybe I shouldn't be so worried. Mom had made it this far without trying something extreme.

Even so, I wondered—what if the unveiling didn't make things better?

Things couldn't go on forever the way they'd been. Or could they?

Second Stratum

6

At 10:15 the next morning I'm sitting in the passenger side of Aunt Erica's old Volkswagen Beetle. Wires hang down all around my knees, and I fear that one false move will disconnect the brakes or something else our lives depend on.

I'm still a little surprised to be here instead of in our family's much newer Toyota. We could have all fit. But Aunt Erica wants to stay upstate overnight, so she needs her own car—and I jumped at the chance to ride with her. I would have done just about anything to avoid sitting in the car with Mom for three-and-a-half hours, but this is an unexpected bonus. I'm eager to catch up with Aunt Erica, who, besides Bradford, is the most fearless person I've ever known. When she isn't teaching high school English, she's off rock climbing or hang gliding or snow camping—and she always lives to tell the story.

"Did you have breakfast?" she asks me, about a half hour into our trip.

I shake my head, suddenly remembering that I

had only drunk a glass of juice before leaving. At that moment my stomach starts rumbling loudly.

Aunt Erica laughs. "Well, there's my answer. I'm famished, too. I'll pull over at the next greasy spoon."

"Do we have time?" I'm thinking about Mom, how worried she'll be if we're late getting to the house. Usually we drive straight through on these trips.

My aunt looks at me sideways, one hand on the wheel. "Phoebe, sweetheart, you have to keep your strength up...especially at times like these."

Her words nestle down inside me, and tears spring to my eyes. I turn away before she can see them.

After a while, we pass a row of signs for restaurants and services. "What about that one, Aunt Erica? Flapjack Heaven, it's called."

"I don't know how greasy it is," she answers, moving into the turn lane, "but I like the name." She pulls into the lot and parks among a sparse gathering of cars.

"By the way, Phoebe," she says as she opens her door, "why don't you drop the aunt thing and just call me Erica?"

I nod, grinning.

"I'm going to make a pit stop before we order," she says. "I'll meet you inside."

Before I get out of the car, my eyes are caught by the stuff in the back seat. I've been so busy watching the road that I haven't noticed how much is crammed back there. Two milk crates and shopping bags are packed to overflowing with clothes and gear. Old, ripped jeans. Thermal underwear tops and bottoms. Blue gloves with the fingers missing. Two yellow crash helmets filled with bags of miniature chocolate bars, the kind you give trick-or-treaters. A pair of ripped-up kneepads. *What's she into now?*

Finally I trudge up the restaurant steps and catch my reflection in the mirrored windows. I can't see a thing—the people, the tables, or jukeboxes—but I know whoever's inside can see me. That gives me kind of a creepy feeling: all those eyes on the other side. Once inside, I see that Aunt Erica is sitting in a booth toward the back, ready for her first cup of coffee.

"Check it out," she tells me as I slide into the seat facing her. "Chocolate walnut. Blueberries and cream. And the world-famous pineapple pizza pancakes."

She hands me her menu, which is at least eight pages long, with four pages devoted to breakfast alone. Suddenly I remember that my wallet is with my stuff in Mom and Dad's car.

"What'll it be?" Aunt Erica says when the waitress comes over.

"Umm...just plain pancakes."

"Isn't that like being offered the moon and settling for Idaho?" Aunt Erica smiles at me, then turns to the waitress. "One tall stack of plain hotcakes," she says, "and one blackberry special."

The waitress scribbles something on her pad, then looks down at me, her head cocked sideways. "Smile, honey. You're such a pretty girl."

"I hate when people say that," I whisper when she moves away. A teardrop falls on the paper placemat.

"Why? You *are* a pretty girl."

"But it's like they're saying you're ugly until you smile," I whisper.

Aunt Erica laughs and squeezes my hand. "That's some pretty convoluted reasoning."

The tears come faster, streaming down my cheeks and plopping embarrassingly on the placemat game, a maze called "Find the Runaway Hot Dog." Aunt Erica hands me her napkin and I dab my eyes with it.

"Phoebe, honey, what's really bothering you?"

I lower my gaze away from her, feeling like an idiot. I scramble for something to explain the tears.

"I forgot my wallet."

"Is *that* what you're worried about?" She laughs, squeezing my hand. "This is on me."

Fortunately the food arrives quickly. She drops my hand—and the subject. I half expect her to bring it up again, to push her point like Mom would, but all she says is, "Dig in."

I don't know what it is—maybe just knowing that I can talk to her if I want to—but suddenly I realize how ravenous I am. I plunge into the pancakes, lavishing them with butter and syrup, savoring the rich mixture of flavors as I chew and swallow. Aunt Erica...*Erica*...is right—sweetness is good, and it has never tasted quite as good as it does now.

"Your mouth is purple," I tell her, giggling. "I wish I'd brought my camera."

She smiles, showing her berry-smeared teeth, then licks them clean.

"So what's with all the stuff in your backseat?" I ask her, taking another too-big bite.

"That's caving gear," she says, her eyes brightening. "Phoebe, it is the greatest. The biggest thrill I've ever had."

"I've read about caves," I say, a little enviously. "All the cool mineral formations. I wish I could see that one in New Mexico. I'm not sure how to pronounce it—Lechuguilla? Anyway, when it was first discovered, the cavers had to explore it naked, because impurities on their clothes would contaminate the pure environment."

"Yeah, I know. Those southern caves are warm enough for naked caving." She chuckles. "But I'd rather have my clothes on. Too many rough edges down below. Plus, our northern caves are a steady fifty-five degrees. You'd freeze."

For a few moments we are silent, and I stare down at my plate, mashing the edges of my remaining pancake with my fork.

"Do you know," Aunt Erica says, "that going underground is a Wiley tradition? Your Mom and I used to be the Adventurers. That's what we called ourselves. We'd take walks near the house and pretend that we were exploring. We found a small waterfall and for a while that was our favorite hideout. But when we came across that abandoned mine—" She smiles, shakes her head. "Your grandmother went crazy thinking we might get hurt. She was right to worry. If it weren't for your mom, I might not be here today."

"Huh?"

"Pam doesn't like me to tell this story," she says, her gaze drifting toward the window.

"Come on," I blurt out. "You can tell me."

"Well, it was in January, the year I turned eight, and two years before Bradford was born. We'd found the entrance to an old mine, just a crack in the side of a hill, maybe a quarter mile from our house, that hadn't been boarded up yet. Your mom never thought we'd fit through the opening, but I proved her wrong."

I grin. "Skinny Wileys."

"We were a lot skinnier back then," Aunt Erica says with a wink. "Anyway, just inside the opening, to the right, was a shaft that was big enough to lower myself into. Pam saw what I was thinking. She pitched a fit and said I'd better not. That was all I needed to hear. In a second I'd climbed right over the lip of that shaft. Your mom was yelling and I was laughing, holding on with my hands. I was going to pull myself back out in a second. Of course, that's when everything went wrong. First my glasses slid off my face, and then I dropped my flashlight. They crashed somewhere below me. I guess I panicked, and I started sliding backward down the shaft..."

Aunt Erica grasps the tips of my fingers and pauses for a moment, letting the suspense build.

"Your mom threw herself in after me, on the rough rock, grabbed me by the arms, and pulled me out. Her timing was amazing. After that, she wouldn't go adventuring with me any more, and Bradford—well, we did some roaming around when he was old enough, but nothing too wild." She shakes her head and adds, "Being a Wiley, of course, he ended up an adventurer anyway. It's in our blood."

A sigh rushes out of me. "I'd like to go caving with you sometime."

"You'd love it, Phoebe. But your mom would have my neck."

My aunt is right, of course. But just for a moment I'd forgotten all about Mom, and what I could or couldn't do. I'd imagined Aunt Erica saying yes, agreeing to take me somewhere wild and remote.

It could never happen. Not even in my wildest dreams.

Unless Mom didn't know about it...

Aunt Erica picks up the check and slides out of the booth. Before she stands up, she looks at me, as if reconsidering. "Someday, we will. I promise." Smiling mysteriously, she flips her sunglasses over her eyes. I follow her to the cash register up by the doors. The cashier takes her twenty and rings up our bill, then he bumps the drawer shut with his gut, a casualty of Flapjack Heaven.

"You have a safe trip," he says, placing the change in her open palm.

7

Grandma and Grandpa's dirt driveway is long, more like a road; it slopes uphill, crowded on either side by thick trees that shield the house from view. I open the window all the way and inhale the smell of sun-baked pine. The memories start coming, still scenes, like snapshots:

Me and Al gathering pebbles in the stream that runs through their backyard.

Bradford climbing a tall tree, coaxing me up after him.

The entire family having a picnic in the field out back, with chicken and lemonade, chocolate cake, and ants, all of us scattered on a patchwork of blankets.

Erica slows down as we approach the house. Eyes closed, I picture Bradford sitting on the porch steps. He always had something to show me—a tiny wild orchid on the forest floor; a bird's nest hidden in fir branches, the tangle of woven sticks cradling fragile, speckled blue eggs. He had a knack for finding treasures in the outdoors, and it delighted me that he always seemed to single me out to share them with.

Yet even here, even during our visits, he could disappear. He would slip off without explanation, to his room or to the woods, and keep everyone, including me, at bay.

"Go away, Phoebe." I remember the sound of his voice, tinny and hollow, and how much the words stung.

I open my eyes as Erica pulls in front of the house. My family's car is parked there, behind Grandma and Grandpa's old station wagon. The porch steps are empty.

"It's so strange not to see him waiting," Aunt Erica says.

My head snaps toward her. "That's just what I was thinking!"

She turns the engine off, and we sit there for a little while. She takes deep breaths; I am barely breathing. I stare at my hands wedged flat between my knees.

"Phoebe." I can tell she's looking at me now. "Your mom told me about that desk. How she wants to sell it..."

I nod, just barely.

"Well, I don't think she really understands you. She's confusing the fact that you were close to Bradford with thinking you were *like* him."

Gently she strokes my hair, once, twice. I want to ask her what she means, but I know that if I let myself speak, or look at her, I will cry. I can't afford that now, before we've even gone inside.

"I'm not a mother, so maybe I can't under-stand…all the worry, all the sniffing for trouble. But when I look at you I see a strong, enduring person."

I'm not, I think. *I'm sandstone. I'm crumbling, and I'm going to blow away.*

Still, I try to hold on to her words, to lock their promise inside me. For a few moments longer, I lean toward her touch.

Grandma Sophie is the first to greet us. I'm a little shocked to see that her hair, which was just begin-ning to gray the last time I saw her, has turned almost completely silver. She wraps her arms around me, and over her shoulder I see Grandpa Ben, stooped and smaller than before. "Look how tall she is, Ben," Grandma says, just like she always does, and Grandpa gives me a broad smile, just like he always does, but I can't shake the feeling that my grandparents have aged much more than a year since Bradford died.

The big Victorian house looks different, too. The living room furniture has been rearranged, and the couches are covered with white bed sheets. That gives me the creeps, though I'm sure that Grandma is just trying to keep the dust off. Like Mom, she is a meticulous cleaner.

Erica comes in behind me and lingers, greeting Grandma and Grandpa with hugs. I move on to the kitchen and duck my head inside the doorway to say hello. There are cups of takeout coffee strewn around the old oak table, and paper bags ripped open, impromptu platters for bagels and cream cheese tubs. Dad and Al are eating, but Mom's bagel is untouched. She gives me a little wave, smiling, as if in relief.

I duck out and head up the carpeted wooden stairs, which creak in all the same places I remember.

Upstairs there are six bedrooms. I head to the door at the end of the hallway and open it. This, the smallest of all the rooms, is the one I've always stayed in. I like its close, cozy feeling, like a mouse hole—and to my relief, I see it hasn't changed. The old wallpaper with its faded design of oranges and leaves still hangs on the walls, and the sheer curtains blow in and out with the faint, hot breeze coming through the window. The same small porcelain bluebird sits in its place next to the books on a wall shelf. I set my suitcase on the bed and open it, unpacking the black dress that Al loaned me, then the black slip-on pumps and black string purse. Handling them spooks me a little; I put them in the closet and close the door.

A few minutes later Al calls me down for lunch. Quietly, I walk back down the hall toward the stairs; I stop at the door of Bradford's old room. I place my hand flat on the wood, as if something of him could pass through the skin of my palm—and then I push it open.

Here too, everything is as it was. The bed is there with its multicolored patchwork quilt, the floor-to-ceiling cases crammed with natural history and sci-fi books, the wire robot he constructed for a science fair.

On a low dresser are pictures in frames: Bradford as a baby; Bradford as a toddler, sitting between Mom and Erica, each of them smiling and holding up one of his hands; Bradford in a backpack on a snow-covered hillside, with an inexplicably joyful expression on his little face. I glance up for a few seconds at my own mournful reflection and then tell him, whispering, *You should be here, with us.*

Now Al is calling me again, impatiently this time. But I don't leave the room just yet. I sweep my eyes over everything in it, and that is when my gaze falls on the locked cabinet beneath the window.

The gremlin closet.

I smile, remembering. Bradford used to tell me his pet gremlin lived inside, and that he had to keep the closet locked or else the gremlin would tear up the house. When I was little, that scared me enough to avoid his room at all costs. But eventually I must have forgotten about this silly story. Remembering it now, I wonder why he'd really kept it locked, what he'd hidden in there. Dirty magazines? Drugs?

When I come back to the kitchen, they are talking about him. Dad is nibbling from one of the many plates of cold cuts, tuna fish salad, and fruit salad spread on the table. Al, with needle and thread, repairs the frayed edge of one of Grandma's aprons. Mom, sitting between Grandpa and Dad, looks at a photo album while Grandma turns the pages.

"His friends Lucas, Roger, and Danny are coming," Grandpa says. "They're the only ones I heard from."

Erica spears a chunk of cantaloupe from a bowl with a plastic fork. "Bradford wasn't much of a people person."

"But they were close to him," my mother insists, her voice strained. "There were his camping buddies, right, Mom?"

Grandma nods. "I think there are pictures of them together, somewhere in this album."

"They were his camping buddies," Mom repeats to Al and me.

A peculiar silence falls over the kitchen. The whining blades of the ceiling fan seem to heighten the awkwardness of the moment.

"You know," Grandma says, "I've been thinking we were wrong...not to have a funeral." When her eyes begin to tear, she shakes her head and breathes in sharply, as if to bring her emotions under control.

"It's okay, Sophie," Dad says. "You did what you thought best." He puts his arm around her shoulder, forgetting he's still holding his fork. A small wad of tuna drops on Grandma's blouse.

"Sorry—" he begins, but Grandma waves him off. She brushes away the tuna with a tissue and laughs a short, unhappy laugh. "That's what I get for taking off my apron, even for a minute."

Dad looks at his watch. "We've got to be at the cemetery in an hour. We'd better get ready."

Grandma's outburst—though it wasn't much of one—has made the air even heavier and thicker than before, and I'm all too relieved to jump up from my seat, even if it is just to go and put on black clothes.

Al stands up, too. "I'll finish this later, Grandma," she says, sticking the needle through the apron fabric. She stoops over Grandma and kisses her, then follows me up the stairs.

"Phew," she whispers to my back. "Was it hot in there, or was it just me?"

I nod, turning to her, and we head together down the hallway.

"So how far is this cemetery? And how long will the unveiling be?"

"I think I heard Dad say the cemetery is ten miles from here," I tell her. "I'm not sure about the unveiling."

"I hope we go home as soon as it's over," she

whispers. "It's creepy, being here. And did you see Mom's face? Her skin looks gray."

Al stops at the door of the room she is using, two down from mine. "Wait," she tells me. "I'll get my clothes and we can get dressed in your room."

Quickly, she grabs her dress, shoes, purse, and makeup bag, then dives after me into my room, throwing all her stuff down on the bed while I shut the door.

"What a great time this is to have my period," she says, mopping her forehead. "All I needed was major cramps on top of everything else. Fortunately, I brought drugs."

I open the closet door and start to pull out my own black things. "Why do you think Grandma mentioned that? About the funeral, I mean?"

Al digs through her bag and finally pulls out a bottle of ibuprofen. "Beats me," she says, twisting and prying open the lid. She gives me a quick glance, then shakes out a couple of tablets.

"I wonder if she really did want one, back then."

"I doubt it. No one did. They were too upset." She pops the tablets in her mouth, then takes a drink from her water bottle.

"That's an understatement."

"Yeah. But I think if it was up to Mom, we wouldn't even be having this unveiling." Al turns away from me, modestly, to snap her halter top off. There are freckles sprinkled across her shoulders, and little rolls of flesh spill over her strapless bra.

"Dad says it's going to be good for Mom," I tell her, speaking low. I pull my tank top over my head. "He thinks things will get better if she can have some closure, as he puts it."

Still turned away, Al slips on the dress she made especially for this occasion, then swings around. It is a simple design with a V-shaped neck. The dark purple fabric blossoming with tiny, dark pink flowers is cut on the bias. Like everything Al makes, the dress is beautiful.

"Do you really believe that?" she says.

I open my mouth, but nothing comes out.

"Mom won't change. She's always going to be more down than up. She has chronic depression—and it's hereditary. My psych teacher talked about it." She gives me a long, knowing look. "That means it's in our genes—the tendency—I don't think I've got it, though."

"I don't either," I tell her, but she doesn't seem to hear.

"Look at Bradford," she goes on. "He was worse than Mom."

I turn away and wriggle into Al's black dress, then take a quick look in the bureau mirror, long enough to see that Al's dress hangs on me like a sack: too big and too short.

"Sorry," she says, watching me. "I should have altered it for you."

With a shrug, I stoop to pick up my shorts, and as I fold them I think of the mirror in Mom's diary. She knew she wasn't supposed to look during shivah, but she did, anyway. I wish I hadn't looked at myself in the mirror right now. What difference does it make, I think, if this dress looks weird? We aren't supposed to care. We're supposed to look to our hearts and not think about appearances. But then I remember what Great-Grandma said about the Angel of Death, about how it might steal your soul if you looked at your reflection.

Al has planted herself in front of the mirror and begun to apply her makeup. Obviously, she doesn't know about any of that.

I feel something hard in the shorts pocket. Digging inside, I pull out the broken halves of the biotite gneiss. Without thinking, I put them in my string purse and snap the clasp shut.

As Al smoothes on lipstick, I wish I could tell her about the diary. I'd like to explain to her how Dad had said Mom was on the right medication now. How I didn't quite believe it. Instead I say, "You remember Mom's cousin, Eli? The one whose picture is on the mantel?"

"Yeah...," she drawls, closing her lipstick. Her eyes go to the mirror again, and she smushes her lips together; only then do her eyes flicker toward me. "Why?" she says flatly.

"Doesn't he look like Bradford? His eyes?" *And he died young, too,* I add to myself. *Does she know?*

"Well, sure. He was probably depressed, too."

Her eyes move away from me, back to her own reflection.

"Girls," Dad calls through the door. "We're going."

My mouth trembles as I step toward her and touch her shoulder. "Did you ever wonder," I say as calmly as I can manage, "if Mom would…"

She shrinks away toward the door. Even though she avoids my eyes, I can see the glint of fear, shiny as gunmetal, in hers.

"If she would hurt herself," I force out.

"Why do you say that?" she mutters, opening the door. She steps out in the hall, and I follow right behind her, about to tell her about the diary, everything I read. Of course, it's too late. Dad looks at us from the top of the stairs, impatient; Mom is just below him, descending.

"Hurry, girls," he says.

Al bolts away from me, and I stand there completely still, whispering an apology. Because I know she can't bear to hear the truth? Or because I can't bear to tell her?

❧

Grandma Sophie beats me to Erica's Beetle, so I find myself squashed between Al and Mom in the backseat of our car. Grandpa Ben sits up front with Dad. The air conditioning is turned up high, but it isn't much of a relief on this roasting afternoon. We ride in silence, past the woods that line the county highway, along back roads with mailboxes on either side, until we come to the high iron fence and gate of Marble Hill Cemetery.

Dad stops at the guardhouse and a uniformed man gives him a map with the Wiley plot circled in yellow highlighter. Grandpa Ben holds the map in his weathered hands so that Dad can see it. We head down the neatly landscaped lanes, past rows of gravesites with tombstones of every size and shape. My palms are sweating, my heart bumping as we go up and down the dips in the road. I clutch my knees to steady myself, ready to hold Mom's hand, to steady her if she needs it, though right now she is using the door for support. Al leans into the other door and her sweaty, clammy arm touches mine with each bump.

Then Dad turns off the main drive onto a narrow, single-lane road, finally stopping close to a large tombstone with the name Wiley on it.

"Oh, God," Grandpa murmurs. Bending his head, he sighs deeply.

"Is that it?" Al says.

"No, honey. That's the old family stone. His…is covered," Dad explains nervously, his eyes darting toward Grandpa.

As soon as Dad parks the car, Bradford's stone becomes visible through the crowd of mourners already assembled at the gravesite. A white sheet is draped over it, not a bed-type sheet, but one made of a kind of shiny, satiny fabric, pulled tight at the bottom. Familiar faces turn as we emerge from the car: Aunt Sarah, Dad's sister, and her husband, Uncle Ron; Great-Aunt Elizabeth and Great-Uncle Joseph; and Bradford's camping buddies, whose pictures I'd peeked at earlier in Grandma's photo album. The rabbi, a small, slight man, comes over to greet us. He embraces Grandma and Grandpa—I can see that Grandma's cheeks are wet—and shakes our hands as we climb out, his grip surprisingly strong.

Mom is the last one to leave the car. At first she refuses the hand Dad offers her and stumbles a bit getting out; finally she relents and hooks her arm through his. I feel a leaden weight in my stomach and resistance in my legs as we walk, slowly, to the gravesite. Grandma and Grandpa go first, then Mom flanked by Dad and Aunt Erica, while Al and I bring up the rear. The other mourners come up to us with a kiss or a handshake, their faces drawn and sad. The plot is enclosed with metal poles and rope, as if there was any doubt where we should stand. The rabbi shepherds us toward the smaller, draped stone.

I saw him, Grace. There, under the sheet.

Mom's words pop into my head and make me shiver. I look at her, noticing how white her skin looks, the frown lines beside her mouth deeper than usual.

"I want everyone to please come as close to the

grave as possible," says the rabbi. "Let us be together, now, as we remember the departed."

A sob escapes Al's throat as she clutches my arm, digging her neatly manicured nails into my skin. Tears cloud my eyes, and I wipe them away with the back of my hand. Grandma and Grandpa, clinging to each other, move forward to stand beside the rabbi, just to the right of the stone. While Grandma weeps openly, noisily, Grandpa holds her, standing straight at attention like the soldier he was once, long ago. My eyes shift to Mom, whose mouth is trembling, and to Aunt Erica, who sobs quietly. I try to pull my arm away from Al long enough to open my purse. It takes some doing, but finally I dig two tissues out, along with one half of the gneiss.

The rabbi speaks a prayer in Hebrew, though he sings more than says it. Several people murmur the words along with him. When he has finished, he steps forward and slowly, ceremoniously, pulls the sheet off the stone.

A fresh wave of weeping rises up. I notice Mom doubled over, touching the ground with one knee, and Dad is bending down beside her. Her forehead drops dangerously close to the ground; alarm rises in my throat as I watch Dad struggle to lift her up.

Somehow, I pull my eyes away and let them rest on the stone. His name is there, engraved in deep, enduring letters. Seeing it, even through my tear-clouded sight, makes the sobs come harder; I clutch Al's arm.

I never cried like this, not even after I heard the news. It's as if the ceremony, the stone, the rabbi's sonorous voice, finally make Bradford's death real. There is no uncertainty about it now: he is gone.

I can't distinguish my own crying from that of the others gathered around me, and somehow that is a comfort to the raw hurt that flows out of me as I read the inscription over and over:

Bradford Jacob Wiley
March 1980–June 2003
Forever beloved

There is some Hebrew lettering beneath that—a translation, I guess—but the thing I focus on is the carving of a bird, a dove with wings spread in flight, at the very bottom. The stone carver must have taken particular care to make the dove lifelike.

I sneak another look at Mom, who is back on her feet, leaning into Dad.

Now the rabbi, in a resonant baritone voice, recites another prayer, first in Hebrew, then in English. I bow my head like everyone else, but I don't really listen, until he chants the ending:

"…Grant perfect rest beneath
The sheltering wings of Thy presence,
Unto the soul of Bradford who has gone unto eternity."

My cheeks sting to hear his name spoken. *It is done,* I think. *He is gone.*

"...And let us say: Amen."

"Amen," I whisper in unison with everyone else; the soothing sound lingers in the air for a long moment. Al loosens her grip on my arm and then squeezes it. I squeeze back.

Then the rabbi says, "There is one more thing we must do. We place stones on the tombstone to symbolize remembrance. This gesture means that we will always remember the departed with love."

Grandma and Grandpa have already picked up pebbles from the ground. Grandma goes first, her face composed, all cried out, and places several of them on the tombstone. They look like quartz pebbles, and they are so clean, I assume they were put there on purpose. Grandpa goes next, and after him, Aunt Erica. Mom hesitates, burying her head in Dad's chest, but he finally picks up pebbles for both of them and puts them alongside the others. Then Al goes, adding hers to the line of nearly identical rocks laid out along the top of Bradford's new tombstone like rough, unstrung beads.

I already have a stone in my hand; just now I realize that I've been holding it all through the ceremony. Stepping up behind Al, I place it at the end of the row: my own memory stone, half the biotite gneiss, broken and beautiful.

8

Back at the house there is yet more food: platters of coffee cake and cookies, pitchers of lemonade. All of us are crowded into the kitchen. I don't know everyone, but I spot Aunt Sarah and Uncle Ron, Great-Aunt Elizabeth and Great-Uncle Joseph. Bradford's three friends, who Grandma insisted come along, linger close to the doorway, too shy or nervous to get a plate of food.

Everyone else, though, except Mom of course, descends on the food like a locust hoard. I never realized mourning could make you so hungry, but it's comforting to eat, to do something that's about life, not death.

Gradually, we move with our plates to the living room, where we sit on armchairs, folding chairs, and the sheeted couches, while box fans whirr away in the windows. After a while, Grandpa clears his throat. He sweeps his pinched gaze over everyone. "Sophie and I want to invite anyone who'd like to...to speak...

about Bradford, some special memory you have of him. He was a unique boy…" His voice cracks and tears wet his eyes; finally he drops down onto the couch beside Grandma. She kisses him on the cheek. "That's okay, honey," she says, and then she surprises everyone with a smile. "You know, Bradford would probably have hated all this attention. He was somebody who didn't want to be fussed over."

"That's true." Unexpectedly, one of my uncle's buddies has decided to speak up. He introduces himself as Roger. He is thin and muscular like Bradford had been, and he seems to have the same strength and ease of movement. "I've never known anyone who racked up more praise from professors, and more near-perfect grades. But he did it all quietly, and if you said anything about it—teased him or just expressed admiration—he'd get really mad." Roger grins. "Once he wrestled me to the ground when I congratulated him on his scholarship."

I hear Dad laugh, and I smile. It's true: Bradford really didn't like to be singled out for his achievements, even though, not long before he died, he'd managed to win a scholarship to study plants in the Amazon.

"As a friend, he was completely trustworthy," Roger goes on. "And he was an amazing outdoorsman. What he understood about survival skills, about how quickly things change in the outdoors and how to respond, was incredible."

"You always wanted Wiley with you out there," one of the other friends adds.

The three guys nod in agreement. From the looks on their faces, they'd all experienced Bradford's skill.

"It's still hard to believe," Roger continues, "that I can't just call him up and say, 'Hey, Wiley, let's go slay the mountain.'"

A few people laugh, and I find myself smiling with tears in my eyes as I imagine Bradford as some big, gangly knight, rushing toward the crest of an Everest-type mountain, doing his best eagle imitation.

I glance at Mom, who sits across the room from me, on a folding chair by the fireplace. She has no plate of food now, only a glass of ice water. There is no laughter in her eyes, no smile. Dad's arm is stretched protectively across the back of her chair. Al sits on the floor in front of their feet, eating potato salad; she looks up, all at once, and meets my eyes. Slowly, she stops chewing and puts down her fork.

Has she seen? Does she understand how bizarre it is that Bradford would catch pneumonia—or that his body, strong as it was, couldn't fight it off? If Roger and the others were with Bradford on his last excursion, why didn't they say something about what had happened? Was it too gruesome a memory to bring up here?

And if they weren't with him, who was?

I want to stand up—to ask someone to set all this straight—but suddenly the questions all jumble together in my mind. It's happy memory time, isn't it? No one wants to hear about the sad stuff or my own stupid suspicions, especially when the mood in the room has lightened.

"I remember," Aunt Erica says, from the arm of Grandma's armchair where she is perched, "a little adventure the two of us had, when Brad was around eleven. You know, he got started on his scientific interests early. He was always begging me to drive him over to the rock shop—once I got my driver's license, that is—but I rarely said yes, because I knew it would take the whole afternoon. But sometimes, I caved in—and in that cluttered place, with its tables piled high with all sorts of rocks from the plainest to the most fantastic—I saw Bradford, my shy little brother, transformed. You should have seen him with his magnifying glass. It was as if he were in some unexplored cave—" She laughs. "Of course, soon enough he was asking me to really take him underground…but that's another story."

"You two," Grandma says, her eyes bright through tears, "were unstoppable."

"We didn't make your life very easy, did we, Mom?" Erica says affectionately.

I see Mom's whole face tighten, and I think of the story Erica told me in the diner, about the time Mom pulled her out of the mine shaft. I guess Mom didn't go on any other adventures with her sister or brother.

After that, a few more people speak, and then the gathering begins to break up. Bradford's friends leave first, then Uncle Ron and Aunt Sarah. A few friends and neighbors stay long enough to say something privately to Grandma and Grandpa, then they are gone, too. The rest of us get busy throwing away paper plates and plastic forks, and Grandma begins divvying up all the leftovers so everyone can take some home.

"Keep them," Mom says. "You and Dad won't have to cook for a few days."

"We couldn't possibly eat it all," Grandma tells her, covering a plate of turkey with plastic wrap. "Besides, we're going away on Monday."

"Going where?"

Over at the table, Grandpa looks up from the newspaper he is reading. "We're going to Florida to look for an apartment," he says.

"An apartment? Florida?" Erica stops on her way to the refrigerator and whirls toward them, spilling some of the lemonade from the full glass pitcher she is holding. *"Why?"*

"This place is just too big for the two of us. It's too much work."

"We aren't as spry as we used to be, either," Grandpa finishes, smiling faintly. "The winters up here are tough on old bones."

The fan blades whirr, whirr through the silence.

Al and I are on the garbage crew—she has put a

fresh bag in the can, and I am in the process of tying up a full bag.

"You can't sell the house!" Erica insists. "We have to keep it in the family."

"Well, that occurred to us, too." Grandpa says. "That would be the best option—except we need money from the sale of this house to buy something new."

"Of course," Dad pipes up. "It makes perfect sense."

"Yes," Mom agrees. "You'll get a good price for it. Some young family will love it."

"I can't believe you're saying that, Pam!" Erica practically spits the words. She finally has the refrigerator door open, and she shoves the pitcher, a little too forcefully, inside. Then she turns to Mom, holding out her hands. "We grew up here. I still love it. Bradford loved it. And I think you love it too."

"I love it," I say, but no one looks at me.

Mom shakes her head, her expression tight, almost like a mask that's about to split open. With a sinking feeling I realize that the unveiling hasn't helped her feel one bit better. I wonder if my clearing out the desk even registered on her radar screen.

Does Dad notice? He sidles up to her and slips his arm around her waist. She looks even thinner next to him.

"All of us are mourning Bradford," Erica goes on. "Selling the house won't take the pain away."

Or selling the desk, I think.

"My mourning is over," Mom says.

"Pam," Grandma's voice rumbles low, like a growl. Erica stares at her sister, incredulous.

"Let's take the garbage out," Al whispers in my ear, and I realize that, like everyone else, I've just been standing there staring at Mom.

"Well," Erica finally says, glancing at Grandma and Grandpa, "I'll come up with the money. I'll buy it from you, and find renters if I need to."

"You're crazy," I hear Mom say as we carry the garbage bags to the cans in the back of the house. I can still hear every word, and they make me cringe: Mom tells Erica she can't handle the responsibility. Erica argues back. Finally Mom says, "I won't be part of this conversation," and adds to Al and me just as we slip back inside, "Get ready, girls. We're heading home soon."

Al sighs with relief, and when I look over at her she gives me a thumbs-up. Then Mom heads upstairs, just a sliver in her narrow black dress.

"Has she been taking her medicine?" Grandma asks Dad in a hushed voice.

"I try," Dad answers, his face lined with worry.

꧁꧂

I change into my shorts and T-shirt, stuff my mourning clothes back into the suitcase, and head out for a walk. A path leads from the back porch of the house, past the cottage. Lawn chairs sit in front and curtains hang in the windows, but there is no sign that anyone has been inside for months. I continue farther along the path, so familiar that I recognize individual trees, boulders, the rises and dips in the path itself. Finally I reach a dry streambed filled with pebbles. They are dull, encrusted with dirt—nothing like the ones from the gravesite. I walk as quickly as I can in this pulsing heat, trying to forget everything, at least for a few minutes.

It doesn't work.

Mom isn't better. That's the bottom line. Maybe she'll pull out of her depression, maybe not. Maybe—the thought darkens my mind—she'll take too many pills again, and maybe this time, she'll get it right.

I think of the diary sitting under my mattress. I'd only read a few pages of it. Suddenly I wished I'd brought it with me, to reread it, to show Al.

Mom will be safe, I tell myself. She has family around her. Despite the sultry heat, shivers run along my skin, and I break into a jog, feeling the sweat pour down my neckline, my scalp. I wrench just enough oxygen out of the air to keep going. But I can't outrun the line that repeats itself over and over, in my head:

Keep her safe.

Keep her safe.

Keep her…

Then I stumble, and for an extended moment I seem to be floating through the air. I'm not even aware of hitting the ground, though once I do, my back throbs.

"Phoebe," someone is calling. "Up here."

My eyes open, but it takes a moment before I can make out Erica standing above me, leaning out over the porch rail.

"Are you okay?"

I nod and raise myself up, first on one elbow, then into a crouch. Now she comes into full focus, and she is smiling.

"You want to go caving?" she says.

Third Stratum

9

Everything happened so quickly, so easily, that I feel giddy thinking about it as I sit in Erica's car, listening to her sing along to a song I don't know.

"'She's all I've got, and gone…'"

We're zipping along the New York State Thruway—as fast as her little car will zip—just the two of us. Free. Maybe only for one day, but free nonetheless. Mom, Dad, and Al headed home yesterday, leaving Erica, my grandparents, and me in the house. Then this morning Erica told Grandma she was taking me for a hike, that she'd drive me home in the late afternoon.

"You lied to Grandma." I fidget in my seat.

"Well, it isn't exactly a lie, is it? We will be hiking, essentially—only underground." She flashes me a smile, as if pleased with herself. It is a tidy-seeming plan, one that, it now occurs to me, she must have hatched after her argument with Mom.

I shift to a more comfortable position. My back is a little stiff from the fall, but it doesn't hurt.

"You okay?" my aunt asks.

"Yeah. I still don't know what made me fall."

"You must have blanked out," she told me. "Probably overexertion."

Was it? I wonder now, because it felt as if, for a few moments, my mind had left my body, gone away from all the strangeness and sorrow of the day.

I turn from my smiling aunt to watch the scenery pass like a movie sequence. I squint my eyes, dry from the wind passing over them, and project myself into the script.

I imagine that Erica and I are on a quest, on our way to search for a rare healing rock. It has been buried for centuries, eluding the many explorers who have come before us. It isn't crystal, the way you'd expect, but a grainy, glinty copper color that seems to glow with an inner light. Anyone who holds it is healed of all afflictions. I play out the movie in my head. When we return from our expedition, science journals compete to publish my report. I win a top prize at the international science conference. Mom smiles at me from the audience at the award ceremony, and afterward, she wears the glowing stone on a chain around her neck.

"Penny for your thoughts," Erica says, reaching over to touch my hair. "What's going on in that brain of yours?"

"Nothing," I mumble, pulling away from her touch and leaning into the car door. *Idiot,* I tell myself. *A healing rock. How pathetic.*

Erica doesn't say another word until we're on the exit ramp. "Phoebe, can you check the map? Is it a right or a left at the T?"

I spread the map out on my lap. It takes me a moment to find where we are. "Go left," I finally tell her.

"Okay. Now, keep a lookout for the Dairy Dip. It's our landmark. And they have the *best* homemade ice cream."

"Mmm. That'll taste good." It is a very hot day, with few clouds to shield the sun beating down on the car roof. I lick the sweat beads off my upper lip.

A truck piled high with hay pulls out ahead of us onto the road, forcing Erica to slow down. For once she doesn't seem impatient. Like me, she is looking out the window. Instead of strip malls, this main drag is lined with farms, small houses, and an occasional business—a greenhouse, a bank, a beauty salon. The houses are set close to the road, and are almost without exception surrounded by neat flower beds and clusters of trees. The fields out back seem to stretch on endlessly. In the distance, cows and horses graze. Most of the houses are decorated with flags for Memorial Day. It looks like the kind of place where people would be friendly, but no one's around.

"Well, look at that. The Dairy Dip dipped."

She pulls off into the parking lot of a low, white-shingled building with no sign on it, just a beat-up awning sheltering some rusted metal tables. The car sputters to a halt and she pulls up the emergency brake. "I was looking forward to a cone," she says with a sigh, then steps out of the car. I get out too, and help her unload the crates and bags from the backseat. She squats amid all the stuff and begins packing two sand-colored army-surplus satchels with miniature flashlights, candy bars, whistles, water bottles, and odd-looking, round metal canisters. Erica packs like a pro—she seems to know exactly where everything goes—as I stand there, hands dangling loose and useless.

"Phoebe, would you grab those boots?" she finally asks, nodding toward the car.

I reach into the backseat for two pairs of hiking boots with socks stuffed inside. The smaller pair is so used that the leather is worn through in places. The larger boots are dark with polish and barely seem broken in. "These aren't yours, are they?" I say, dangling them in front of Erica.

She turns, shading her eyes with her hand. "Nope. They're your mom's."

"No, they aren't. I've never seen them."

"Probably because they've been in my closet for years. I don't even remember how they ended up with me."

"Did she ever go caving with you?"

"Oh, no." Erica shakes her head vigorously. "She might have done some hiking—the aboveground kind—when she was in college. But as you can see, she didn't exactly wear 'em out." She points to the crate filled with clothes. "Here, would you sort these clothes for size? There's one set for each of us."

"There's a set for me?"

Again she stops what she's doing and gives me a mysterious smile. "Let's just say I've got some buddies who are around your size."

I smile back, feeling a surge of pleasure that she had thought of me as someone she could go caving with. Still, in this weather, it seems a little nuts to be making piles of long underwear tops and bottoms, jeans, and flannel shirts. I finish just as Erica is tightening the buckles on the two satchels. "Here," she says, handing me one, then pointing to a yellow helmet lying on the ground. "You can take that, too. It's got an adjustable band on the inside." Then she loads the mostly empty bags and crates back into the car. "We'll change in the woods," she says, grabbing her clothes, helmet, and one of the satchels. I watch her walk across the parking lot and up the low ridge that marks the beginning of the woods. She disappears into the dark, inviting shade beneath the green leafy trees. *She's really, truly nuts*, I think, laughing as I grab the helmet. Inside the brim is a white label with bold blue printing:

THE GLOW STONE

Wilderness Rescue Corps.
Call 1-800-RES-CORP.

I plop it on my head—I'll adjust it later—and pick up all the junk that Erica has left lying on the ground. At last I head off after her, eager to get out of the sun.

At the top of the ridge, I stand looking into the forest. She is nowhere to be seen. A trilling of cicadas ripples through the treetops. I walk a few yards into the woods. That's when I spot her in a nearby clearing, stripped down to her purple bra and red underpants. I practically hurl myself—and my armful—into the clearing.

"Hey! Someone could see in here!" I shout.

She laughs, raising her arms overhead to reveal the dark, unshaven tufts, and she slips into her long underwear top. I can see that her legs are hairy too. "No one's around," she answers confidently, as soon as her head pops through. "But if it makes you feel better you can watch out for me, and when I'm dressed I'll do the same for you."

"Forget it. I'll just wear what I'm wearing. It's at least eighty-five degrees."

"Spider, it's a steady *fifty-five* underground, remember? Plus it's damp. You need the layers—especially the polypropylene underwear. It'll keep you warm and wick the moisture off your skin."

"So what's with this 1-800 number inside the helmet? Are there pay phones in the cave?"

She laughs, shaking her head, and continues to dress. When she's done, she sits down on the pine needles, facing the parking lot. "Go ahead," she says. "I'll keep an eye out."

I sigh heavily and pick up the long underwear top, dangling it between two fingers like a dead fish.

"Smells good here, doesn't it?" she says, inhaling deeply. "I love the scent of pine."

Finally I have everything on except my socks and boots, and I start to fold the clothes I was wearing. My hand feels a lump in my shorts pocket—the other half of the biotite gneiss. I turn to see if Erica is watching, but she is completely focused on a new task. It looks as if she is playing with sand, pouring it from one small metal canister to another.

"What's that?" I transfer the gneiss into my front jeans pocket.

"Carbide," she says. "It'll be our lifeline underground."

I swallow, feeling a twinge of uneasiness. "What do you mean, lifeline?"

She stops what she's doing long enough to touch my knee. "Relax. People have been using it for hundreds of years. And for my money, it makes the best light to cave by. Much better than the electric headlamps most people use these days."

Inexplicably, Erica leans over and spits into the carbide-filled canister. I'm about to ask why, but check myself, figuring that her answer probably won't prove very reassuring. "Who taught you how to use it?" I ask, watching her fill another cylinder with water from a water bottle.

"My caving buddies." She screws the water cylinder onto the one containing the carbide. "They call themselves 'The Rock Chompers.' Kind of serious about it. They loaned me all this equipment."

"So I guess you know what you're doing."

"Enough to guide you on a short caving experience. Here, want to light it?" She hands me the disposable lighter. "I spit on the carbide to create acetylene—this is the actual gas that allows you to light the lamp."

I nod. "Uh huh."

"And this pointer controls the height of the flame. You want to keep it low—about an inch and a half—to help conserve the carbide."

I nudge the sundial-like pointer with my finger, but it barely moves. "How long will a full canister last?"

"Oh, about three hours. We'll only be down for half that time, though. And we'll have extra cylinders and backups just in case."

"Backups?"

"The mini flashlights. You should never depend on them, though. If they get wet, they're dead. But these carbide babies can withstand being dropped, rained on, and trampled." She raises the lighted lamp and snaps it into a circular metal disk.

"A miner's lamp," I say. "Awesome." I watch her put the whole contraption onto a bracket in front of the helmet.

"You can light it now. Go on."

I flick the lighter at the small hole on top of the water canister, following the process in my head. Water drips onto carbide. Gas forms. Add fire, and bingo. The smell of dust and lime fills my nostrils as I move the lighter away and look for the flame. It is miniscule, barely visible in the daylight, but then Erica turns the pointer and the flame rises higher, into a thin white, steadily burning column.

"That doesn't look too strong," I say.

"It's because we're outside." She turns the pointer again, making the flame disappear. "But you'll be surprised. In the dark, between our two lamps, we'll have enough light to see by."

"What if we get separated?"

"We won't." She looks at me point-blank and closes her hand around my forearm. "The first rule of caving is...never cave alone."

10

So what's rule number two?" I say when Erica returns from putting our regular clothes in the car. "All cavers must resemble overdressed gnomes?"

"Always." She grins as she sets her helmet on her head.

I adjust the band of my yellow helmet and put it on, too. My head tips forward with the weight of the carbide lamp up front.

"I recommend you leave your watch," she says. "Could get smashed." She stuffs hers into her satchel.

"I'll take my chances," I say, tightening my wristband a notch as I check the position of Minnie Mouse's arms. "That way we'll know when to come out." It surprises me to hear a tremor in my voice.

"Phoebe." Erica turns away from buckling her satchel and looks up at me. "I've done this route a bunch of times. It takes an hour and a half, max—the perfect length for a first-time cave experience. You wouldn't want to stay down any longer than that."

"Why?"

She hesitates before answering. "Your body cools down quickly and there's no sun to warm you up." She smiles. "But we won't be down there long enough to worry about exposure or hypothermia."

I shrug, determined not to let my fear show. "Glad I asked." But all at once I'm thinking of a story I read in the newspaper, about some kid who got separated from her Girl Scout troop on a camping trip. About how it rained all night and her core temperature dropped, and how she was dead by the next morning.

"The darkness is absolute, Phoebe," my aunt goes on excitedly. "No sun. No stars. No light at all except what you carry—" She touches the front of her lamp. "—so there's no day or night, in the technical sense. It's an opportunity to step outside of time."

A breeze disturbs the branches overhead, too high up to cool us off, then dies down again, leaving a deep silence in its wake. I sit on a rock and put on the boots; with the thick socks they fit pretty well. I'm about to stand up when I get this crazy thought: *You could tell her…now. "I found Mom's journal."*

And I could go on. *"Did you know about Mom? Do you think she'd try again?"*

Just thinking about it gets my heart racing, and I know I can't, I won't say it aloud—because the words would sound too real.

It's a relief when she says, "Ready?" and all I have to do is answer "Yeah."

THE GLOW STONE

She finishes buckling her satchel and tells me to follow her. After around fifteen minutes of hiking in the woods, I'm lagging behind. I'm used to running on a fairly level surface in sneakers, not trudging over rough ground in heavy boots. Erica sprints on ahead of me, pumping her arms and kicking out her legs with each step. Soon we're yards apart on the narrow trail, no more than a rough notch lined with broken boulders. At one time it might have been a streambed. Now it runs along the forest floor like a scar that never healed.

"Slow down, Erica Wiley," I yell when she is out of sight. I run, sweating, until I reach a bowl-shaped dip in the earth, almost like a dried-out swimming hole. At the bottom Erica sits cross-legged beside a rounded pile of stones. A perfect slide-show photograph—but I have no camera.

"What are you doing down there?"

"We're here!" she shouts.

"Where?" I shout back, eyeing the steep inner curve of the bowl. The next thing I know I'm doing a ski-slide down it, letting out a warrior whoop as I land on my butt beside her. "I think I just mashed all my chocolate bars," I tell her, peeling the satchel from my back.

"Doesn't matter. They'll still taste good."

I tuck my legs up under me and begin to strip off the flannel shirt.

"Don't," she says. "We're about to go under."

"Under?" I follow her gaze to the rock pile, which I see now isn't an accidental arrangement. Someone deliberately placed it at the edge of a small, smiling crack in the earth.

"We'll have to light our lamps before we go in." There's no way a human being can squeeze through that narrow opening, but her tone is matter-of-fact. Completely deadpan.

"You're joking, right? We can't fit through there."

She answers with another one of those smiles, mysterious and a little teasing. "This is where being a skinny Wiley really comes in handy."

She stands up and suddenly the air is filled with the sound of cawing and flapping—she's startled a crow out of a pine tree overhead. I watch it fly off, the adrenaline racing through me. Erica dips one boot then the other into the opening. I have the impulse to run and grab her, but my body is unmovable, thick as poured lead. She feeds herself into the hole, her chin tucked in, her helmet wobbling a little on her head, and lowers herself until she is chest deep. At that moment I unfreeze, lurching forward in panic to grab her by the shoulders—an unnecessary rescue, since at that moment she somehow propels herself out of the hole and onto her butt again.

"Voilà!" she cries, raising both arms overhead. "Zee human gopher!"

I clap for her like "zee human seal," but my heart does a crazy hopping dance. "You're insane." I laugh weakly.

"But see? Not a scratch."

I sit beside her, cross-legged, taking deep breaths. Erica's clothes are covered with dirt. She is grinning from ear to ear, but I can see the concern in her eyes as she places her hand on my knee. "I scared you, didn't I?"

"A little," I admit.

"There's a natural ledge just beneath the hole. As soon as you scoot in, you can sit right down on it." Then she adds gently, "I was scared the first time, too."

I stare at the narrow aperture in the ground, no more than a shadow really. As much as I'd read about caves and imagined exploring them, I never thought I'd actually have the chance. Now that it's happening, part of me can't believe it and part of me wonders if I'm brave enough.

"We can go back," she tells me now. "Or take a hike. Whatever you want."

My gaze shifts to her face, suddenly serious and still. Whatever you want. An unsettling sensation rises up in me, a mixture of dread and excitement and queasiness.

"No," I tell her, "I still want to go in."

"Okay," she says with a little hint of pride, though I sense she would have been fine with whatever I decided. "Here, I'll light you. Then I'll go in, and in a minute or two you can follow."

I don't pull away as she reaches up to my helmet, turning the dial until the pungent, almost vinegary smell is released. She flicks her lighter and I hear a slight whooshing sound. "There. You're all set. Just keep this tucked in," she says, tickling my chin playfully as she tightens the strap. The part of me that is still afraid wants to scream, but all I do is grin. It seems as if everything is happening in slow motion: Erica lowers herself into the narrow hole until only her helmet and shoulders are visible, then tucks in her chin and goes under. I wait on my hands and knees, staring into the pit as her yellow helmet is swallowed up by the pitch darkness.

And now it's my turn.

At first I manage okay, simply imitating her magic trick, dipping one boot in, then the other. I stall by tightening my watchband and checking Minnie Mouse's hands. Eleven-twenty. Finally I take a few deep breaths to stave off panic, but as I begin to lower myself, my fear rises. I don't dare go past my waist, but I can't push myself out either—and now my arms begin to tremble from holding all my weight. *In or out,* I tell myself, imagining Erica sliding away into the darkness. Finally, I tuck my chin in and slip under.

"Did you find the seat?" she asks from somewhere below me, her voice tinny. I have found it—a bumpy ledge that my butt can barely fit on.

"Just sit and look down, Phoebe. The passage slopes to the left."

I can barely see my boots, much less a passageway, but all at once I begin to slide. Pebbles plunk down on my helmet and I grab the strap of my satchel before it slips off my shoulder. I hear the soundtrack playing in my head, a rising trill of violins as the heroine gathers a little speed, too surprised to scream or steer. Fortunately, there is only one way to go down the chute, which feels roughly as long as two playground slides.

Moments later I land on my feet, and I turn to see Erica standing beside me. For a split second our beams collide and I shut my eyes against the blinding brightness, but the impression of her skeletal face, with dark eye sockets and nasal holes, lingers behind my eyelids. When I open my eyes again, the brightness fades and her profile comes into view—real, live flesh, not bone.

"After the first fifteen minutes," she says, "you'll forget there's a world aboveground."

"Whoa," I say, shivering. "I don't know if I like that idea."

We stand there, staring into the open, endless-looking space. Within moments, I begin to make out the faint contours of walls in the distance—shadowy, colorless walls holding up all that earth and rock above our heads. Logically I know it won't all come crashing down. I'm also fairly certain that the faint hum in my ears isn't voices whispering in the silence, and that the tingling all over my skin doesn't mean I'm disintegrating. Laughter bubbles out of me.

"What's so funny?" Erica says.

"All of this."

She smiles at me, her teeth sparkling like bits of quartz in the artificial light. "Now tell me, would a hike in the woods have been this interesting?" She puts her arm through mine and pulls me forward into the dark, our boots crunching the loose pebbles or whatever's coating the ground. Then she lets go of my arm and walks on alone. After a few paces she stops and stands very still, as if watching or listening for something.

"Never...cave...alone," I call out ominously, adding plenty of gravel to my voice. She turns her head. In the light of my lamp her profile looks hard, solider than skin. "Just joking," I add.

She turns away again.

"So what are you doing?"

"Getting my bearings. It's been a while since I was here last. Help me look for a landmark."

"Why?"

"We'll be exiting the cave somewhere else, but still, it's always good to know another way out."

I start to shiver again. Why should we need another way out? I don't ask the question, though, because I don't really want to hear the answer.

Slowly I turn, shifting from foot to foot the way Erica is doing, looking for some outstanding feature in the gloom, but nothing is visible that even faintly resembles a landmark.

Then something flashes in my eyes, a golden glint.

I squint along the beam of light, breathing shallow to keep the white puffs of condensation from rising up and messing with my sightline. A jagged form appears—a large, yellow calcite tooth—its surface sparkling in the lamplight. I walk toward it and reach out to touch its moon-cold surface. With a kind of awe I realize that it is right beside the passage we just came through. I stick my head up inside the opening, looking for a speck of sun or some other sign of the world above. There is none.

A hand touches my shoulder, startling me. I'd almost forgotten Erica was there.

"Here's our landmark," I tell her, patting the tooth.

"Hey, that's a good one! Now don't forget to look back and fix it in your mind."

But after walking a short distance, when I finally remember to look back, I can see neither the tooth nor the passage out.

11

Walking passage," Erica calls. Maybe she can stand upright in it, but my helmet knocks against the ceiling and I have to bend over. The water from my lamp drips down my nose. In some places, the rock walls come so close together that I'm tempted to walk sideways. The rock scrapes me through my jeans and snags my shirt.

"Can you hear that?" Erica's voice startles me. I can't see her, but I know she is somewhere up ahead in this narrow passage. I make myself go faster to catch up, and around a bend, I bump right into her. "Hear what?" I ask.

She bows her head and points at the rocky path. I giggle, uneasy with the knowledge that Erica might not only be hearing things, but seeing them, too. Then it sneaks up on me: the burping, bubbling sounds of water somewhere beneath us.

"Follow me," she says. "It's the only way to get the full effect."

And so we walk. The noise grows louder. She pulls me closer to the wall, demonstrating how I should keep my back flat against it, moving sideways like a crab. I follow her a few paces until she stops, taking my bare hand in her gloved one. The noise is now a low roar, and the path trembles slightly, shaking my boots.

I feel as if there's a taut wire running through me from head to toe. At any moment it could snap. I might go insane.

Erica points her finger downward, and I look. Our lamps illuminate a ravine inches from our feet; the light glints off the water far below. I stumble backward, pulling her with me.

"It's all right," she murmurs. "You won't fall in."

Still, I grasp her sleeve as if she might run away from me—or vanish into thin air. There are dark streaks on her cheeks and forehead, like tribal markings.

"What is it?" The roar of the water nearly drowns out my voice.

"A subterranean river." She smiles, still holding my hand, and leads me farther along the path, where we can hear each other better. "Know how caves form?"

"Yeah, I've read a little about it."

"This bedrock is all limestone," she says, sweeping her arm in a wide semicircle. "Most northeast caves are."

I nod. "It's a carbonate rock, water soluble."

"Right. So when rain falls, it carries carbon dioxide from the air into the ground, and over a long time this dissolves the rock. Groundwater and rainwater form springs underground."

"So why aren't we swimming right now?" I ask, half playfully poking her in the ribs. "How do you know which passages are clear and which are filled with water?" Uneasily, I imagine trying to swim weighted down with all these clothes and equipment.

"Well, it's been a dry spring," Erica explained. "When groundwater levels fall, the passages are apt to be dry." She grins. "With a few exceptions."

I follow the dim, bobbing halo of Erica's helmet as she takes the lead again. The path widens, the walls retreating so far back that the greenish limestone is only barely visible. The river noise has faded to a faint buzz that pulls on my eardrums, and the air is heavy, humid. Every so often I stop to tap my boot toe against the path, testing its solidity beneath me, as if it could easily shift and give way at any moment. In a place like this, anything could happen.

"Have a seat," she says when I catch up with her.

She's already seated on one of several stones scattered around a huge, pewter-gray, flat-topped boulder: a Stone Age picnic table. We're in the middle of a crossroad. Three paths, much narrower than the ones we've been walking on, branch out ahead. I sit on the stone closest to hers and watch her turn her satchel over, dumping a landslide of miniature chocolate bars onto the slab. "Have some," she offers. I take a Snickers, my favorite.

"Are you cold?" she asks, unfolding her map.

"A little."

"We won't be here long. I just want to take a reading." She unwraps a Milky Way and shoves it into her mouth, chewing as she consults her map. Then she leans toward me until our helmets clack and presses her finger to the paper. "We are here."

Bowing my head, I look at the black lines that seem to shift in the flame light, and finally make out a round circle with several tiny shapes inside it, one of them an oblong like our table slab.

"And," she continues, sliding her finger maybe an eighth of an inch, "we're headed here."

I squint harder to read the tiny black print. "Pictograph Crawl?" I say with a grin. "Sounds like some prehistoric dance step."

She laughs. "The rocks have pictures on them. You'll see. After that we'll head out of the cave."

"This way, right?" I point to a line that continues on from the Pictograph Crawl to a tiny circle marked EXIT in bold letters. The entire journey spans the length of my fingertip.

"You've got it." She nods and slips her arm around my shoulder, giving it a squeeze. "Here. You can navigate us out."

"Oh, goody," I say, putting the map in my satchel.

We sit there a little longer, our breaths condensing into little clouds, and my thoughts drift back to the unveiling. It occurs to me that at this moment we are way deeper underground than Bradford.

"That was a pretty stone you left for Bradford," she says, quietly.

My heart jumps. Has she read my mind...again?

"Was it one he gave you?"

I nod, touching my pocket, relieved to feel the other half still there.

"Mmm," she says. "You know, I'm usually not one for all these rituals, but that is one I like. Bradford would appreciate a gift of stones."

"Yeah," I agree, "though he might have thought the quartz pebbles were a little boring."

She stops repacking her satchel and looks at me through the opaque breath puffs. I see she is smiling, as I am. "You're right. He would." She shakes her head, still looking at me. "You really knew him pretty well, didn't you?"

I look away, into the endless dark. "I thought I did," I mutter.

Erica sighs. "He was hard to know. Very complex."

"What I don't understand is..." My voice trails off and I swallow, trying to gather courage. "How could he have gotten himself into that situation, in that storm? You heard what his friends said...how skilled he was outdoors."

My words vanish in the cave quiet.

"Yes," Erica begins, but says nothing more.

"I found Mom's old diary." The words pop out of my mouth and hang in the air between us—air that I now suspect contains truth serum.

"She wrote about your cousin, Eli," I rush on. "He died about the same age as Bradford, didn't he?"

"Younger. Seventeen." Her voice is clipped, tense. She stands and readjusts her helmet.

"I know I shouldn't have read it."

"Phoebe—" Erica fiddles with her lamp, tipping it downward so that the beam first shines on my boots, then back up to the level of my chin. "We should get going. Keep moving."

"How did he die?"

She takes a step away from me, then stops. "Phoebe—" She turns, looking just to the side of my face, so that her light won't blind me. "Some things are better left in the dark." She coughs. "It's a matter of survival."

"How?" I insist, knowing that it's useless. She won't tell me. She walks away, her quick steps echoing softly behind her.

As I follow her, the meaning of her words begins to take shape in my mind. Is it better not to know? Is that how Erica survives? It seems so strange to me. She seeks out dark, dangerous places—but she doesn't get sucked down into them. She just passes through.

All at once I understand. Mom's illness, the one that Bradford also had and that I now suspect Eli had too, hasn't touched Erica.

As for me...

My steps have slowed, as if I can't walk any faster than my groping, grappling thoughts. Images swirl around in my head, the suspicion growing stronger each moment.

Eli didn't die from natural causes.

And neither did Bradford.

12

rica is facedown against a wall, her arms and legs splayed out like a criminal about to be frisked. She doesn't seem to realize I'm standing a couple of yards away—or maybe she is simply ignoring me.

"Hey!" I call out.

"This is going to be really interesting," she says. From her absorbed tone, she might be talking to herself. I watch her hand, then her arm, vanish into the wall.

I come closer, close enough to see that this is not a magic trick. There is a tunnel, kind of a large borehole in the middle of the wall, and she is feeding herself into it. In moments, all that is visible are her boot soles. "Hey!" I yell again. "What are you doing?"

With a grunting, X-rated noise, Erica frog-kicks the rest of herself into the hole.

"Stand back! You might get kicked!" Her shouts are muffled, but still forceful. I can hear her breathing hard. "Wait till...you can't..." The rest of what she says is unintelligible.

Fine. Do your little adventure thing, I think, as I lean against the wall to wait. *Just don't take forever.*

From my vantage point the underground room looks endless, the dark deeper than any I have seen. Anything could be out there. I search for a land-mark—something, anything, to fix on—and then I notice, maybe twenty feet away, a cluster of mustard-colored stalactites hanging from the ceiling like muddy icicles. These, I know from a book I read once, are mineral deposits created by water dripping down into the cave, but somehow, just then, they seem like works of art.

I turn the beam of my headlamp away from the vastness and point it again toward the hole, wonder-ing, suddenly, if Erica's already out the other end. She said to wait, but how long? I'm not sure I can do this. But what if she doesn't come back for me? What if she's stuck and *can't* come back?

Shuddering, I force myself to take a deep breath, and I climb in on my belly, wriggling like a snake. The pebbles grate my skin, bruising everything they touch—hands, elbows, stomach, hips, butt. I curse aloud, something I hardly ever do. I wish I'd put gloves on like Erica told me to. Fortunately, I listened to her about layering my clothes. Without the mira-cle underwear and all the other padding, I'd proba-bly be bleeding all over, not to mention freezing my butt off.

I raise my head higher, bumping the ceiling with my helmet, and I taste dirt. But I can hear Erica ahead of me, grunting and kicking, and it keeps me going: the last thing I want is to be alone in this place.

The tunnel twists, narrows, forcing me to flip onto my side, which makes slithering almost impossible. Still I squirm forward as best I can. Finally, when the tunnel widens out again, I lie on my back, breathing hard, water from my lamp dripping down onto my face. And that's when I see it: a red-brown horse outlined in black, legs stretched in a run, head twisted back over its shoulder, its hide rippling in the sputtering lamplight.

"Phoebe, you okay?

Her voice startles me—I hadn't realized she was so close. I try to move, but my hands are pinned beneath me, trapped. My breath comes harder, faster, until I think I'm going to hyperventilate.

"Calm down, sweetie. You're almost there. I can see you."

"But I can't *move!*"

"There's a handhold behind your head. Pull on it."

I bend my head back and see that she's right. Just past the horse is a ledge that I can grab, if I can figure out how to free my hands. But there is no wiggle room here—I can only lift my hips straight up. With every last ounce of my energy, I raise my body and inch my hands out, creeping them up the tunnel walls and back behind me, feeling around. At last my fingers find the ledge.

The lamp flame sizzles. I imagine it flaring up, engulfing me, burning me to a crisp. The next thing I know I'm pulling like crazy and pushing with my feet. Then I feel a tug. Erica has grabbed a chunk of my shirt and is hauling me out.

She drags me like a rag doll, props me against a wall. I inhale close, sulphury air, feeling the pinpoints of pain where the pebbles had dug into me. A sound gurgles from my throat out into the air, low and strange.

"Are you all right?" she asks, her face so close that I can see dirt caking her fine cheek hairs. Apparently satisfied that I haven't croaked, she leans back against the opposite wall, but keeps her eyes on me, her boot soles touching mine. The space we're in is an igloo-like limestone shell with a crack across its ceiling that resembles a long, jagged mouth.

"Here. Sip."

She hands me her water jug and I take a swig. "Spit," she says, but I've already swallowed, my whole face puckering at the gritty taste. "It's better to spit first, before drinking," she explains. "Did you see the pictographs? The horse is more visible than the bison. Some art teacher made them back in the fifties."

"B.C. or A.D.?" I say sarcastically. Relieved as I am to have come through the meat grinder in one piece, I'm not exactly thrilled that we suffered all this agony to see some cave paintings created fifty years ago. I stare at Aunt Erica in the shifting light, wondering if I can really trust her judgment.

She laughs giddily, in a way that sounds a little forced, and taps her boot soles against mine. Then she grabs a candy bar out of her satchel and throws it in my lap. This time I tear the wrapper with my teeth, not even caring that I swallow paper and dirt with the chocolate. I crave the comforting sweetness.

"That was the hardest part of the cave," she tells me. "You did great."

I wish I could let it all out—my anger at being forced to do something so difficult, my fear at being left. But I hold it in because I also feel strong—tough, even—and surprised at how much her admiration means to me.

She leans in closer, peering at my face, though I doubt she can see my conflicted expression. Faces are difficult to read down here, with all of these tricky shadows.

"Erica—"

"Shh…honey, be quiet now."

"About Eli…and—"

Bradford's name is about to leave my lips, when she places her fingertip over them. "Wait," she whispers. "This is where I wanted to show you the cave. Really show you. And to do that, we need silence."

The distraction catches me off guard. Before I can say another word she reaches for my helmet and turns the dial on my lamp all the way shut, then does the same with her own. The afterglow stays in my eyes even as the darkness presses in, filling everything.

I take in a lungful of stinky air and start to cough, convulsively bending over, panic pressing into my midsection like a steel plate. It is several moments before I can breathe again, and when I straighten up, I see nothing.

"Aunt Erica!" I don't see the fun in this. Maybe I should have gone home with my parents.

"Shhh. Just listen."

"To what?"

She has disappeared. I raise my hands in front of my face, but they are gone, too. For experiment's sake I shut my eyes, and it makes absolutely no difference. Another laugh ripples the air. It sounds like mine, but seems to come from all around me, from the cave walls. Then I simply listen to the sound within the silence, a faint, steady hum, now higher, now lower. It is as if there is something the rocks want to tell me—if I can just listen more carefully, if I can forget to be afraid that they'll swallow me up. Am I strong enough to stand this? Or will I really break down, mind and body dissolving into the dense air?

Aunt Erica gives a little sigh and scrapes her boots against the ground. I hear the click of the lighter and see a living face loom up before me.

"Congratulations," she says. "You're the first Wiley in your generation to come through that."

Come through what? I want to ask. *The tunnel? The complete darkness?* My thoughts tumble over themselves, and at the bottom of it all is a kind of dumb amazement that I'm still sitting here, that I haven't vanished.

She relights our lamps, motioning for me to crawl out ahead of her. Finally, I shake off my stupor and creep back into the narrow tunnel.

"Look up," she says after we've been writhing for what seems like forever.

Painted on the limestone ceiling is a barrel-chested bison, its horned head pointed downward. Its ribs are painted on a wavy surface, its rump on a rounded one. When I shift my head and study it from a different angle, it doesn't really look like a bison at all, but a dark stain on the rock.

The next moment, the flickering lamplight makes the animal seem to be running. It reminds me a little of Mom's paintings, which are filled with hidden images. That's what I like so much about them, I realize. Look at a waterfall, and you'll find a woman's long hair. Gaze at a door and you'll see a goldfish embedded in it. Sometimes you can't tell if the trick is in your own eyes or on the canvas.

Maybe Mom *is* an adventurer—in paint.

I look back at the bison and watch it moving, galloping, fleeing deep into the folds of limestone where no one can find it.

13

I didn't plan to do it, to go off on my own, to break the first or any rule of caving. One moment I was standing around, waiting for Aunt Erica to come back through another crawling passage. The next moment I wasn't.

※

She has found another tunnel just beyond the Pictograph Crawl, one that isn't marked on the map. "I'd like to pop in there and see if it goes anywhere," she says. She sounds as excited as if she's just won the lottery. "What do you think?"

I shake my head. "I'd rather not."

"Okay." She seems disappointed. "We'll keep going."

"You go," I urge her. "I'll wait here."

After a moment she says, "You sure?"

"Yup." Already I've stationed myself to the side of the hole, back to the wall, in watchman mode.

"Well…"

She shifts from foot to foot as if considering, then opens her arms wide and pins me in a great bear hug. "Phoebe Bernstein, you are wonderful!"

I take in the momentary warmth of her body, then push her away, toward the rabbit hole. "Go, before I freeze my buns off."

She drops onto her knees and looks up at me one more time before she feeds herself into the hole. "See you in a couple of minutes," she says, her voice already sounding remote.

Twice she calls back to me, twice I answer—and then, I don't hear her at all. The couple of minutes stretch out unnaturally long, and then I hear it again—someone calling my name:

"Phee-bee."

This time, the voice clearly isn't coming from the hole. It sounds too expansive, too echoey. It seems to be coming from a passage to the right of me. A walking passage.

How did she get there? Was the crawlspace short, looping around into the bigger passage? Did she just want me to know that she was okay? Or did she want me to follow?

"Phee-bee."

Maybe it's another one of her tests, I tell myself, like the Pictograph Crawl. Will I be the first in my generation to explore this new passageway?

The thing is, I'm not even sure that it *is* Aunt Erica calling me.

"Phee-bee."

I stand there a little while longer, stalling, rubbing my hands for warmth, even though I know what I want to do.

I follow the voice.

Fourth Stratum

14

I am confident, kicking my legs out in big long strides. My body warms up quickly and I keep going, occasionally stumbling over little stones in the path, but making progress. I stop and look around. Isn't this the passage that curves back to the saber-tooth rock, the tunnel out? I had tried to observe everything carefully, as Aunt Erica had told me to do. I start walking again, less confident now. The passage meanders gradually around a bend, beyond which I cannot see.

The voice I was following is gone.

I break out in a sweat, my heart pounding in my throat. *Where is she?* Have I wandered farther away from her, instead of getting closer?

"Aunt Erica!" I scream. The echo vibrates in my ears for a long time afterward, and when the silence fills in again, I listen. The only sound I hear is the faint burbling of the river. I stand still for a moment until the shivers begin again, and then I walk back— I think—the way I came.

"Phee?"

The voice is faint, barely audible, but it's enough to make me stop short and yell again. "Aunt Erica! I'm here!" The echo responds, then the silence settles over me again.

"Phee!"

The voice propels me toward it. "I'm coming!"

But I haven't bargained for the split in the path that rushes at me now. Why didn't I notice it before?

"Which way?" I shout. "Right or left?"

Two descending paths branch off to either side of a narrow wall of limestone.

"Oh please, God," I say aloud. "Let her be close. Let her bring me out again, into the sun—"

The sound of my own voice jolts me. I've never really prayed before, not like this, from the pit of my fear-wrenched stomach.

The shivers return, but not her voice.

Warm tears run down my face. I swipe at them with my fingers, brushing dirt into my eyes. Now I'm blinking and crying both—and stumbling around in a circle.

The chills grow stronger. Even stamping my feet doesn't seem to help. I manage to blink most of the dirt out of my eyes and peer down the two passage-ways. Should I take one of them? Or just stay still and wait for her?

It's the cold that finally decides. I have to keep moving, to keep warm. I pull the map out of my satchel and squint at the lines, trying to trace a path from the Pictograph Crawl to this fork—but I'm too cold, too panicked to really make sense of things. I'll go to the right.

But how will she know? What if she comes this way and can't tell which path I've taken?

A note, that's what I need. Maybe I could tear off a corner of the map and leave her a message. I scrounge through my satchel, hoping that Aunt Erica slipped a pencil inside when I wasn't watching, but I guess she didn't think I'd need one. Anger tightens my throat, tasting dry and ashy. *She should have thought of everything.* When I cram the map in my pocket my fingers scrape against the broken biotite gneiss. I pull it out and try to mark on the cave wall, but it only makes faint scratches on the damp rock. No one would ever see them.

Then I notice something about the gneiss that had never occurred to me before: it is roughly triangular in shape, almost a pointer. I kneel and place the stone on the cave floor so that it is pointing down the right-hand passage, praying that it will catch Aunt Erica's eye when she comes looking for me.

Walking at a brisk pace takes away the shivers. At least I was right about that. And I know I have to keep warm at all costs.

The river sound grows louder and louder. I listen to its complicated music, hoping to hear my name. I force myself onward, wishing again that I hadn't resisted the gloves Aunt Erica had tried to push on me.

Suddenly something whizzes past my head. An arrow?

It comes past me again, accompanied by a tiny, high-pitched sound.

I back up to the wall, looking out into the passage so I can see whatever it is the next time it passes. Nothing happens, and I reach down to get the water bottle out of my satchel. But instead of touching canvas, my fingers brush slick, oily fur.

I imagine myself screaming, flailing around, like the heroine in some horror movie. I must be standing still, though, because the creature continues to cling to the side of my satchel, calmly it seems, one wing tight against its body and the other extended slightly. My light shines through this wing, and I see that it is delicate and beautiful.

Gently, I lift the strap from across my shoulder and hold the satchel at arm's length, watching the bat. Is it sleeping? Resting? Or is it sick, infected with rabies? Gasping, I drop the satchel, and watch the creature take off, winging away with a faint squeal.

Was that the noise I was hearing and not my name at all?

I feel a weight in my belly. Part of me wishes the bat would come back, even though it frightened me. At least then I wouldn't be alone.

Eventually I stop to take the map out again. I study the thin, tangled lines that indicate the maze of paths down here. For the first time I notice that there are three different entrances to the cave. *Why didn't she tell me?*

My eyes fall on "Pictograph Crawl" near the middle of the map. I move my finger to the entrance closest to it. At its bottom is a small, round, jagged shape—the gold tooth? —but I can't tell which of the paths I'm on now. This thin, spindly one, its end shaped like a question mark? Or the longest one, made up of braided lines that stretch all the way to the other end of the cave? According to the map's key, it is two and a half miles long. Wavy lines—water—run beside it.

I can hear the river more clearly now. That settles it, I tell myself, shoving the map back into its plastic bag. I must be on the right path. The river had been about this loud on the way in, too. I start walking faster, swinging my arms, my satchel going forward and back like a pendulum.

The carbide flame illuminates the widening, downward sloping path in front of me. I remember what Aunt Erica said about carbide light—it doesn't project very far, but spreads out, allowing a greater range of vision. Diffuse light, she called it. Suddenly I wonder: am I burning too much? She said it should last three hours. I take the watch out of my satchel and check Minnie's hands—it is one-thirty, about two hours since we entered the cave. So there should be another hour's worth. And now I remember that there are refills in my satchel.

I won't need to refill, though. Aunt Erica will find me before another hour is up. The cave isn't that big.

Just as I'm telling myself all this, I trip and pitch forward. The satchel flies off my shoulder, arcing in the air, its strap waving momentarily before I land belly down. I cry out as my chin hits rock and my helmet jams forward, the chinstrap excruciatingly tight. Water sloshes out of the lamp, splashing on my fingers. Pain shoots from my forehead all the way deep into my neck, and I cry out. My teeth crunch down on something wet and gritty: blood mixed with dirt. I hear the river talking loudly below me and I breathe its cold, metallic smell.

For a while I just lie there, groaning softly, eyes shut against the pain. It isn't only my head, but my right hip that is killing me. Something's wedged against it, sharp as a knife.

Idiot! I shout at myself. *You weren't paying attention!*

Sweating, I inch forward on my stomach and crane my head toward the stream. Flecks of light play on its surface.

Keeping my movements gradual and small, I roll onto my side and push myself to a sitting position. I examine what is under my hip: a ridge of rock, not even very sharp looking, but obviously sharp enough. I look around for my satchel but don't see it.

Again I point my headlamp toward the stream below. There's the satchel, crumpled on the rocks.

I realize that if I'd fallen differently, I'd be down there now, too, battered and broken.

What was in that satchel? Carbide refills. Lighter. Flashlight. Water bottle. Candy bars. Map. Wristwatch. Whistle.

At least my memory isn't gone.

Hot tears well up. *Don't start now.*

I take the helmet off. Sweat has plastered my hair to my head. I turn the lamp dial so that the flame shrinks to barely more than a spark. I'll have to start conserving carbide now. Who knows how close I am to running out?

Please. Let the fuel hold out. Let there be a way down to the river.

I dig inside my pocket, forgetting that my gneiss is gone. It would have been a comfort to hold it in my hand—a feeble connection to my old life.

I gaze down into the crevice one more time. The flickering light is too weak to let me judge width or depth, so I hang my head over the edge for a better look. It strikes me that there is a way down to the stream, thanks to my long, spindly arms and legs. All I need to do is make a bridge of my body spanning the crevice and lower myself downward, inch by inch.

But what if I'm not strong enough?

I shake my head. "No," I say out loud. "I need the stuff in that satchel." My voice is strong. I take that as a good sign.

"Go, Phoebe," I whisper, and slide over the edge.

15

I must look like a crab, back pressed into the near wall, feet against the far wall, and the rest of me a taut, trembling cord. If I relax, even for an instant, I risk falling onto the rocks below.

The stream is talking to me. It could be telling me how to save myself. Or how to let go, so it can finish me off.

I drop one heel—an inch, max. Then I wriggle my back down to keep my body level. Drop the other heel, slide down again. Something sharp scrapes the skin of my lower back. I cry out, fighting the tears that begin to cloud my sight. I can't afford to lose it now.

Drop heel. Wriggle. I keep at it even though it is agonizingly slow. I'm too far from the ledge now to go back up.

I turn my head, lamp water splashing on my cheek. The stream is very close now, only about a leg's length below me.

And then the cord snaps. All the tension drains from my legs. Spider's bridge is falling down.

❧

I must have blacked out for a while, or gone into some sort of temporary shock. Maybe it's true that the mind tries to protect itself by shutting down when the body is in great pain.

The freezing water revives me, slapping at my back, pulling at my skin and clothes. Black-silver water, so cold it feels hot. My lungs are so tight I can barely breathe.

It takes a moment to figure out where I am and how I got here. Then it hits me. *Moron,* I think. *Was all this worth some stupid satchel?*

This must be the scene where the heroine cracks:

She is sitting in the middle of a frigid-cold stream on rocks that could have broken her, and she's laughing her head off.

No. Wrong emotion. There is nothing funny happening here. The director—whoever that is—wants tears, but his heroine cannot cry. The laughter has emptied her out.

Then she catches sight of the satchel, swelled with water but intact, caught between two upright slabs of limestone at the edge of the stream. She staggers to her feet and inches her way toward it with small, sloshy steps. The water freezes her butt and other places she didn't know could be frozen. The shivers come in long waves, making her double over to puke, but nothing comes up. She gropes for the next rock—and something closes over her hand.

Flesh.

She looks up into a pair of gray eyes. They are so familiar that she lets herself be pulled out of the water.

The young man's long arms hang loose at his sides. "You can't stay in those clothes," he says.

Abruptly she backs away, shocked as much by the sound of his voice as the idea of stripping. She stands there, frozen to the spot, and gapes at him.

He is wearing an olive green shirt, clean chinos, and sneakers. He has no helmet, no warm layers, no caving gear.

And he looks just like Bradford.

I'm no longer shivering now but shaking. My teeth are chattering uncontrollably, the cold pouring over my skin in icy waves.

"You could die." His voice is insistent, though not alarmed.

"I'll work on the bag," he says. "You get dry." He

brushes his hair out of his eyes, just like Bradford used to.

I know it's rude to stare, but I'm afraid that if I look away he might disappear. I watch as he retrieves the satchel from the water and tries the clasp. "Sticky," he says.

No, I tell myself. *It can't be.* I back away, eyes always on him, and bump up against a stalagmite. Turning, my lamp illuminates a field of these spiky, oddly beautiful formations sticking up from the cave floor.

I glance back toward the river. He has the satchel open and is laying out its contents on the dry ground. I see him sniff the last Snickers bar, closing his eyes as if in a reverie. I turn away, stumbling into the space between two stalagmites—not exactly a dressing room, but it will have to do.

Chills buck my entire body. I strain to loosen the wet bootlaces enough to pull my feet out, then strip the waterlogged wool socks off the miracle sock liners, which are only damp to the touch. The same is true of the long underwear beneath my jeans. Removing my helmet, I set it on a ledge at chest level and yank the soaked flannel shirt over my head without even bothering to unbutton it. I breathe out a sigh to find that my miracle top, too, is only slightly wet.

Stomping around, shaking my arms and hands, I try to bring some warmth back into my body. It's then that I'm aware of a presence behind me.

Startled, I turn to face him. He holds the satchel out to me. "You should refill your lamp for the way out."

I reach for the satchel strap, staring at those slate-gray eyes.

"Nothing was lost," he says, sitting on a boulder.

I set the satchel on the ground and crouch beside it. Then I begin to take out what I'll need to relight the lamp. He's right, I see. Nothing is lost, nothing ruined. I turn on the mini-flashlight and then shut the dial on the carbide lamp to kill the flame. Touching it, I singe the tips of my fingers and cry out. He looks over at me. "Still hot," I say.

"You heard me, didn't you?" he says, his mouth edging into a smile. "When I called."

"That was...you?"

He laughs. "Why are you so surprised, Phoebe?"

"I thought it was Aunt Erica."

"No you didn't."

He's right again, of course. The voice hadn't sounded like Aunt Erica's, but I'd followed it anyway.

"Phoebe," he says. "You know who I am." The laughter's light hasn't entirely faded from his eyes.

All I can do is stare up at him, taking him in.

"You will make it. Your mom is afraid you won't, that you're too much like me. Or Eli. Or... her..." He lowers himself to the ground and sits cross-legged like I do, his knees just inches away from mine. "But you and I both know better."

I nod slowly, remembering that Aunt Erica had said almost the same thing. I shape his name with my mouth. *Bradford.* But I can't quite bring myself to say it aloud.

"Mom...she tried once," I finally say, looking up to meet his eyes. Now I see the bits of variation— tiny, golden brown cracks within the gray.

"Yes," he says.

My gut feels like someone has grabbed and twisted it. "Will she...try again?" I whisper.

He doesn't answer at first, and the beating of my heart sounds so noisy within the cave silence. Finally he answers, "I don't know."

I start to reach for his hand, but something holds me back. I couldn't bear to discover that he's not real, just a hologram or an image from a movie. And then I feel his arm around my shoulder, pulling me in, holding me as I cry.

"Why can't you tell me?" I say. "Why?"

"Phoebe... Phoebe," he repeats in his quiet, soothing voice.

"What about her painting? That helps her, doesn't it?"

"Yes."

"But she gave it up."

He shrugs. "All the reminders."

"Reminders?"

"Like your desk, and the upstate house. They remind her of her pain, so she wants to get rid of them." I feel his grip on my shoulder relaxing. "She can't. She can sell them, lock them away—but she can't forget them."

Tears make warm, wet, stinging paths down my cheeks.

"And Phoebe? Remember, the desk is yours now. She won't sell it unless you want her to." He looks away from me, then back. "Didn't you find the note I left in it? I broke the lamp when I went in there, and the biotite gneiss—"

"B-Bradford."

"I didn't mean to break them," he continues. "But—I wanted you to know it was me, that I was there."

"Bradford."

"Now we've got to get you out of here," he says. "Can you light your lamp?"

I cannot focus on his words, only on the question gathering in my mind.

"Can you?" he repeats.

Inhaling deeply, I reach for my helmet and hold it in my hands. I know I must ask it now, though dread runs white-cold through my veins.

"You...you didn't have pneumonia, did you?"

He takes the lamp off its bracket, studying it, seeming to ignore me. I'm pretty sure he's heard me, though it's hard to read his expression. His features are less distinct in the beam of the flashlight.

My hands shake as I unscrew the lamp's canister

and fill it with fresh carbide granules. I spit in the canister, close it, and then relight it.

The flame rises. I pick up the helmet and turn the light toward my chest, as if to thaw myself out.

"Good thinking," he says.

The flame, though bright, gives little heat. I move it around in front of my torso, holding it as close as I can to my body without setting myself on fire. After a while I feel a little warmer, and I offer him the helmet, but he shakes his head no.

We study each other, silent inside the silence. My chest feels on fire now with the lantern's heat. Bradford crouches low, so we are eye to eye. All the warmth that has built up in me drains away suddenly, and the shivers start up again. He doesn't look quite real anymore. His skin appears illuminated, like a paper lantern. His laugh lines are gone. His laughter. I listen harder, as if that will somehow bring it back. But it's gone for good.

Still, he speaks. "Why do you think they didn't want a funeral?"

I try to say his name, but can't get it out. He seems to be crumpling. I set the helmet down and crawl toward him, and then I hear myself singing: *Don't cry, sweetie pie. Don't cry, light of my eye.* It's a song Mom used to sing to me. I reach out to grasp his hands, to cradle them in mine, but he yanks them away and lumbers to his feet, walking backwards up the steep stream bank.

"Will you forgive me, Phoebe?" he calls back.

I start after him. "For what?" I manage to ask.

He holds up his hand, stopping me from coming any closer. "Go now," he says. "Leave your wet clothes here. Take that path"—he points farther up the bank, toward the left—"and when you pass the tree roots, look for the tunnel out."

"Is it on the map?" I ask desperately. I can no longer distinguish him from the darkness.

"Bradford!" I scream, panicked. "Don't go! Come with me!"

And then, when he doesn't answer: "Don't do this, Dr. Gloom! Don't send me away!"

Finally I hear him. "Rely on your compass," he calls back. "It's more dependable than a map."

"I don't have a compass!" I shout, stumbling after him, reaching for him.

My arms gather air.

16

radford. He is gone, absorbed into the damp spongy air. I gaze at the place he'd been standing, as if I could somehow rearrange the molecules to make him reappear. Acrid-tasting bile rises in my throat. I gag, then pitch forward onto my knees. I am as pitiful as a lost dog.

I tip back my head and study the crevice above me. Its walls are impossibly straight. Did I really come down that way? Did I really think I could go back up? Weird sounds bubble into the air. "What a fool," I say aloud, laughing at the sound of my own voice. It's so useless. *Could have died. Will die. Now. Here. Alone.*

I drop my head and begin to cry. Lamp water drips down my forehead, mixing with tears, and finally it is this, the threat of losing light, that gets me back up to my feet. My head and all my limbs are humming with fright.

Have to get dressed.

I look back at the spot where he'd been standing, and beyond, to the shadow-drenched field of stalagmites. Even though I was just there, it appears unfamiliar. I stumble upward to search the spiky forest for my clothes.

Yes. Here they are, the wet jeans and socks. But the miracle sock liners are dry, and the shirt is only damp. I struggle into it, buttoning it all the way to the top. My feet in the liners slide around in my mother's boots. I throw the satchel across my shoulder and weave around the formations, heading, I think, in the direction Bradford pointed.

At first it feels good to move, to pump my arms and legs, to warm up. The path is level, more or less, and my freshly filled lamp burns brightly. But then his words echo in my head—"Will you forgive me?"—and I start to shiver all over again.

Maybe I will find him. Maybe he will change his mind and come with me.

That hope pushes me along the upward climbing path, which grows narrower and steeper with each step. A breeze plays with my flame, making it smoke. Between this and the carbide fumes, I can't seem to get enough oxygen. I cough until the pain burns my throat.

Now I can see them, over a rise: a mass of dead tree roots suspended in the air, tangled up with their shadows, which shift like spindly arms. A moment later I make out actual arms—human arms—moving inside them, and the outline of a head, a torso.

My heart smacks against my ribs: Is someone in there? Do they need help? And then I see gray eyes, hands, a flash of silver.

"Bradford." I exhale his name.

He doesn't respond, doesn't seem to even know I'm there. He seems to be in a fascinated trance, fixated on the silver thing. I squint my eyes to try to make it out. Is it some chunk of mineral he's found? He passes it from one hand to the other, as if weighing it, testing it. I can see that it's not much larger than his hands. I think I see him scratch it, once, with his fingernail.

He might be performing a magic trick, turning the rough mineral chunk into something smooth... because now I can make out a sleek, shiny barrel...a trigger...

"Bradford! No!"

Still, he doesn't hear me.

I grab the roots, shaking them, clawing the rough knobs until my fingers are bloody.

I can no longer see him. And I know now with a sickening certainty that he will not come with me.

17

I step back until I'm an arm's length from the dried-out, dirty roots. Nothing's there. *See? You imagined it. The whole thing. You've been hallucinating.*

But that seems, to my mixed-up mind, only half true.

Got to move. Find the way out.

That is the one thing I'm sure of. Bradford said so.

For good measure, I take a swallow of water to soothe my parched throat and throw the last Snickers to my empty stomach.

Frantically I search the widening passage for an upward climbing tunnel, a pinprick of light. I reach for the map, practically tearing it down the middle as I yank it open, and try to focus on all those snaky lines long enough that they'll stop writhing on the paper. All I can really make out are the names: Pictograph Crawl. Hell's Chamber. Heaven. Breakdown.

Breakdown—ha! Hilarious little mapmakers.

Letting the map fall, I try to jog around the passage,

but I merely stumble, an unmerry-go-round horse. Cold sweat covers my face.

This must be the end of the movie, when the heroine realizes she was never in any real danger. A sunlit tunnel opens overhead and she floats up through it.

The End.

The next thing I know I'm down on the rough, pitted floor, coughing, trying to breathe. I'm no heroine. Not with lamp water trickling into my eyes and each breath a stab to my lungs.

But there *is* a light overhead—a light!

I struggle onto my knees and wipe the water from my eyes. *There it is.*

Dizzy, I try to stay very still, to focus on the sun-filled rock. It is glowing, practically translucent, like amber. It hangs from the ceiling of a warm-looking shelter in the cave wall just a few feet over my head. Above and to the right of the little cove is a nearly vertical tunnel, the source of the light that spills down into it.

This must be the way out that Bradford described.

But I'll need to rest up before I can manage the tunnel. If I climb up to the shelter and lie down for a minute…

Staring at the spot, I see myself very small, a baby, tucked up in Mom's arms as she walks me around and around. "That is the sun, Phoebe. This is a tree. This is a rock…" Her voice is as soft as the scuttling clouds that move across my eyelids.

Now I see something else: a closing door. I lean out over the side of my bed after Mom has tucked me in, just to make sure she won't shut the door tight but will leave it cracked so I can keep my eyes on the night-light out in the hallway. It is punched with tiny stars that help me sleep....

No. Don't sleep yet. Stand up.

It takes me a long time to struggle to my feet, but once I am more or less standing, I see that if I want to get to the shelter I will have to climb a wall twice my height.

I place my palms on the moon-cold rock, fingers testing the depth of the gashes that scar its surface. None of them seem deep enough to grab hold of with the toe of my boot. And even if they were, how could I boost myself up there? I have no energy. I can barely lift my feet.

"Aunt Erica!" I shout. Pain grips my lungs, my vocal cords. I realize now that I haven't heard her voice since she disappeared into that last crawlspace. *What if she didn't make it out, isn't looking for me? What if she had an accident or—*

I shake these thoughts off. She has to be okay. Has to be.

What would she say to me now?

"Climb, Phoebe. Climb however you can. Get up to the sunlit rock. Then you can rest, gather strength for the tunnel out."

Yes. That's exactly what she'd say.

I smile for a moment, resting my cheek against the

wall, hearing Aunt Erica's warning in my head: *Never cave alone.*

But I'm alone now.

Several feet away, I spot a small spur of rock around hip height. I edge closer and see that it is nearly the width of my boot. After a few tries, I step up onto it, turning my torso so I can feel around the pocked limestone over my head. My hand finds a dent—not much of one, but it will have to do.

One...two...

Just before pushing off, I lose my handhold and fall backward in a spray of lamp water. I close my eyes, trying to sense what is wrong with me. But I can't get past the pain. It is all I can do just to breathe.

I can't die here.

Bradford gazing at the silver pistol. Mom uncovering the mirror. My rocks in the desk—dirty, musty, jumbled. These images float through my head like tiny rafts. "Will you forgive me?" he had asked.

"No, forgive *me*, Bradford," I wail. "Forgive me. I couldn't save you."

I am crying now.

"Bradford, I forgive you."

I've been tired for such a long, long time.

I force myself to focus on the amber shelter above me. It looks warm. Squinting, I make out a solid mineral ribbon suspended from the ceiling, its light and dark stripes all in motion, rising and falling like waves. Waves that will carry my pain away.

I see Bradford patting his chest.

Rely on your compass.

I know what he meant now. He wasn't talking about a real compass, one you can hold in your hands. He meant something inside me.

⚜

My determination flickers like a flame, bright and promising, warming me, then it dies back.

I fumble for the satchel clasp and dig out my Minnie Mouse watch, holding it up to the lamp. Minnie's arms poke through the shattered glass. There is no telling time now. Somehow, that is a relief. I feel my breath grow slower; I stare at the rippling waves above me until the watchband slips through my fingers.

⚜

I awaken in a fuzzy, semiconscious fog, my body crumpled onto itself, a searing pain moving up my right leg. I open my eyes enough to see that I've fallen by the wall—the wall I was going to climb.

No chance you can make it up now, I tell myself.

But if you don't, you'll die.

"No," I say loudly, to put an end to these thoughts. I fight to keep my eyes open, not to drift away again.

The pull is so strong…stronger than I am…
No!

My eyes jolt open, but quickly close again. In the darkness that follows I see my desk with all the drawers pulled out, and the rocks still inside them, neatly arranged on their cotton batting. They let off a resplendent light.

I go through the drawers one by one in my head, remembering as many of the rocks as I can, visualizing their names printed on the small cards. Feldspar. Quartzite. Illite.

Their light grows brighter…hotter…igniting inside me like a campfire, beating out the pain, making me burn instead. How can I go from cold to hot so fast?

I curl up even tighter, into a ball, to hold the flame as close as possible and never let go. I see myself small again, hanging backwards over Mom's knees like a bat, as the world goes upside down.

"I won't let go," she promises. "Not unless you tell me to." But she loosens her grasp a little, enough so I feel the scratchy rug against my scalp.

Then that memory vanishes too. I keep holding on as tight as I can to what is left of the flame, a little ember fighting off the great cold.

Fifth Stratum

18

Cocoa steam—that was the first thing I remembered—sweet steam warming my cheeks. Someone holds a cup to my lips and cradles the back of my neck. Lights crisscross my face, so bright I can't open my eyes.

"Sip," I hear someone say.

Bradford?

A drop of the warm cocoa slides onto my tongue.

"Phoebe, can you hear me?" says another voice, this time a woman's.

Erica?

"Phoebe," the voice repeats, "I'm Dixie Callahan. I'm a paramedic. We need to get you warmed up before we put you on the stretcher."

I shake my head. I want to speak but I can't make my mouth work. I can't ask the question that I need to: *Is Aunt Erica okay?*

"We're going to get you to the hospital," says the woman. "Your aunt is waiting there for you."

Relief washes over me and I breathe a bit more deeply. I might even be crying a little. My whole body shakes. I am colder than I've ever imagined possible—except for my right leg, which feels as if it is on fire. Someone lifts the helmet off my head and replaces it with a much more comfortable fleece cap.

As I drink, the shivers grow less. The pain in my leg begins to dull. Thoughts form in my mind, then slip away.

I hear Dixie speaking to the man who gave me the cocoa. "Careful with her leg, Bob," she says. I groan when they lift me onto a hard stretcher and wrap me in blankets that crinkle as they tighten the straps around me. There is some kind of hard cushion or restraint around my head to keep me from moving it. I feel myself rising slowly, and they slide me onto a shelf of some kind.

Up until then my eyes have been firmly shut. Now they struggle open, shedding tears that had collected under the lids until I am able to see the formation suspended inches above my nose. I can make out the ribbons of translucent mineral interspersed with darker bands of rock. My healing stone glows with a warm light.

"Waking up?" a man asks.

Then I hear Dixie's voice close to my head.

"We're going to lift you out. It may be a little bumpy, but we'll try to make it as smooth as possible."

"Am I okay?" I mumble.

"Yes," she says. "Thank goodness your aunt called as quickly as she did. She found a house near the place where she exited the cave."

"We tried this sinkhole first," Bob explains. "It's the easiest way into the cave. What a stroke of luck that you happened to be here and not near one of the other entrances." He shakes his head.

"What amazes me most," Dixie adds, "is that, even in your condition, you practically got yourself out."

I try to tell them what happened, though apparently none of it makes much sense to my rescuers. In my head, though, it's all very clear: How I followed the voice and found Bradford. How he saved my life by showing me how to take care of myself after I fell in the stream. How he pointed the way out.

My eyes drift shut again. I hear Dixie say that the painkiller is starting to kick in. Someone else mentions my broken ankle.

That, to me, is the strangest thing of all. How could I have come through all this with only a broken ankle? It seems like such a small price to pay for getting out alive.

I want to tell them about the gun, how fixated on it Bradford was, and how he had told me to go away.

Was that what was in the locked cupboard in his room? Was the gremlin his gun, locked away, waiting?

But what I most want to say I can't tell to these people who don't know me or my family.

I would have to give up trying to keep Mom safe, because I couldn't.

It was up to her.

Maybe it's the painkiller, but all these thoughts that I can't speak soon fade into blackness. Wrapped tight in that cocoon, with pairs of hands lifting, steadying, pulling, and pushing me, I surrender myself to the care of these strangers.

⚜

The next thing I remember, I smell sun-warmed pine and see overhead a rock dappled with leaf shadows. The rescue team pushes me up out of the hole into the beautiful, clear, late-afternoon light, and places the stretcher flat on the ground.

I stare at the circle of pines that poke the belly of the sky. Rays of sun filter low through the trees. Is this the same day as when I went into the cave?

I start talking again, asking questions. "Does Mom know I'm okay? What about Al and Dad?"

"I'm sure your aunt called them," Dixie says, squatting down beside me. She strokes my forehead. I'm surprised to see that her hair is streaked with silver. She and I seem to be there alone, but then I see, hovering above us, the faces of the other people who'd come for me—exhausted but content, as if their ordeal had been worth it.

"I couldn't bring him with me," I blurt out.

Worry creeps into Dixie's face. "Who, honey?" she asked. "That Bradley you were talking about?"

"No, no, Brad*ford,*" I tell her, shaking my head within the restraint. "He made me go away, so he could—"

"Sometimes, hypothermia makes people hallucinate," Bob says. "It sounds as if you were seeing things."

"No." I shake my head. "He was there."

"You might have *thought* you saw someone," Dixie explains gently, "but no one was actually there with you. Your aunt said it was just the two of you, and as far as we know, no one else was down in the cave today." She smiles. "Now, there's an ambulance here that's going to take you over to the hospital, and you'll see your aunt."

"Wait—"

"Shhh…don't worry, Phoebe. You're going to be fine."

I know I'll never get them to understand about Bradford, but there is one thing I can do. "You saved my life," I whisper. What more can I say? "Thank you" seems as weak as their carbide flames out in this natural light, but I say it anyway, lacking any other words.

"Phoebe, we're just glad we got here in time." Dixie leans over and kisses my cheek. "You're welcome."

They bear me up the bowl-shaped rise. Already I

can see the flashing red lights. Maybe there will be something I can do to let them know how grateful I am—later, when I'm strong again.

For now, I let myself be carried.

19

Red lights pulsed through my dreams and gradually muted into a bath of whitish-green, where I floated for an age, deeply asleep, yet aware of still being tethered to the earth, to life. When I finally woke, I saw a white cast on my lower right leg and foot, suspended in traction above the bed, and a small, scarred hand closed around mine on the blanket.

"Aunt Erica?"

She had been waiting. She leaned across me, a little stiffly, and gently clasped my shoulders. When she pulled away, I noticed tears in her eyes and a scattering of scrapes and black-and-blue marks on her face. Her wiry hair, matted with dirt, was clipped up on her head. "You look terrible, too," she said, and I laughed along with her. Then we simply looked at each other, grinning in mute amazement.

I made it, I thought. *We both made it.*

"Really, though, how are you?" she asked.

It took a moment to answer. Where to begin? "Alive," I finally said.

"Oh, yes." Still grinning, she poured water from a Styrofoam pitcher on my bedside table. "Here, drink. You're dehydrated. See, they're pumping liquids into you."

Aunt Erica pointed to the IV bag hanging overhead, and my eyes followed the clear tube to the needle stuck in my right arm. I winced, though it didn't really hurt. I drained the cup and held it out for more.

As my aunt poured another cup, I looked at her more closely. Something seemed different about her, beyond the obvious signs of having been in the cave. She seemed older, and less like the carefree sprite I was used to. There were dirt-encrusted worry lines across her forehead and a downturn to her lips, as if she were concentrating a little too hard on what she was doing. "Phoebe," she said, her gaze settling on me. "Where'd you go? Why didn't you wait for me?"

I looked away, out the darkening window. The sky was a dusky blue-purple, and the streetlamps around the parking lot below were coming on one at a time. "I...I heard something," I said. "Someone calling."

"I did call out a few times," she said. "I was hoping I might find more pictographs, so I stayed longer than I intended—but I couldn't have been gone more than five minutes altogether." She paused. "Then I came out, and you were gone."

Ellen Dreyer

I only half heard her. I was trying to figure out what was bunched between my legs. Was that a bandage? Did I hurt myself there too? Then it hit me.

"I got my period," I announced.

Erica nodded distractedly, not realizing the significance of my words. She was still waiting for the answer to her question. But to me, getting my period was one more amazing thing that had happened over the past ten hours. And—I smiled to myself—it was one thing Al couldn't tease me about again.

My aunt pushed herself up out of the chair and crossed the room, her steps dragging more than usual. From this distance, perched on the wide windowsill, she looked back at me.

"Aunt Erica—"

"I just don't understand," she said. "Did you think I'd leave you there?"

I swallowed, hard. "I know you must be really angry with me. I'm so sorry I went off like that...for all the trouble I caused."

"It was a pretty stupid thing to do." Her fingers were wrapped in the blind cord, and she was pulling the blinds up and down a few inches. "But I don't blame you, Phoebe. I take responsibility for everything. I had no right taking you down there in the first place, without asking your parents...and certainly not the day after the unveiling."

I shook my head. "But I *wanted* to go! I told you I did!"

She walked back and sat on the bed next to my good leg.

"I chose to go caving, and I chose to go off, away from you."

"You have to let me take responsibility for this."

"No—"

"It won't wash with your mom."

"Where *is* Mom?" My heart raced with the thought of seeing her.

"On her way up."

"Now?"

"Of course. Wild horses wouldn't keep her away." She smiled wryly. "And she certainly doesn't want *me* in charge."

For the first time since the cave, I felt as if I might puke. "Al and Dad, too?"

"Yeah. And Grandma and Grandpa are coming over from the house. They'll be here any minute."

I breathed deeply, trying to calm the churning in my stomach. "Does Mom know about—" I pointed at my right leg.

Aunt Erica looked away, shaking her head. "I didn't think it was wise to worry her over a broken ankle. And besides, I didn't think you'd want me to tell her."

She was right. This was what we did in our family. We lied to Mom, presumably to protect her. They lied to Al and me, trying to protect us from the truth about Bradford's death. The lying had been going on for a long time, even before Bradford died. And now I saw that my brave, adventurous aunt, the person I'd always admired and wanted to be like, wasn't really trustworthy either. By lying, Aunt Erica hadn't taken responsibility at all. The churning in my stomach wasn't nausea. It was anger, the same anger I'd felt in the cave when I asked her about Bradford and Eli.

My gaze wandered to the windows, now dark. "Why didn't you tell me the truth? Why didn't you tell me how Bradford and Eli really died?"

Hesitantly, she reached for my hands, which I thrust beneath the hospital sheet, out of her reach. This hurt her, I could tell. But I was tired of being kept in the dark.

"Phoebe, you know...your mom wouldn't want me to talk to you about it. I think you should ask her." Her weary voice was barely above a whisper.

"Mom? She lied to me, too. To Al and me."

"Your mom..." She never finished the thought. Her eyes drifted away, back toward the window, as if she wanted to fly right out of there.

The door opened and Grandma rushed into the room. "Oh, darling," she said as she leaned over to kiss me gently on the cheek. "Thank God you're all right." She cradled my head, stroking my hair, and I gave in to her gentle touch that reminded me so much of Mom's.

My grandmother moved aside so Grandpa could

stoop to hug me around the shoulders. He held me carefully, as if I were made of eggshell. "Oh, Spider," he said. "We're so glad you're all right."

The two of them hovered over me. They hadn't even acknowledged Aunt Erica, who was eyeing us warily from across the room.

"I'm going to tell them the truth," I blurted out to her. "I'm going to tell them everything."

"What truth?" Grandma asked.

"That we went caving, first of all, and that I chose to go off on my own. That I'm to blame for what happened."

There was so much emotion in my voice it startled everyone, including me. Grandpa took a step back, and he and Grandma looked at each other, confused.

"We knew they found you in a cave," Grandpa said. "We talked to one of the rescue workers—I think her name was Dixie."

I nodded.

"She said you were mumbling a lot," Grandma put in, "about...some very strange things."

"Because of the painkiller," Grandpa finished, and cleared his throat. "You need to rest now. We'll talk about all that when you're feeling better."

I wish it were as simple as that, I thought, looking at them, wondering how I could possibly explain.

They were plainly still worried, all of them, even though I'd made it through alive, even though I was okay. Of course, they hadn't seen what I'd seen. We sat in an uncomfortable silence that seemed to stretch on forever, and at last I dozed off.

When I next opened my eyes, I looked directly into Mom's. They were so much like Bradford's had been—slate gray, like the sky before a snowstorm.

She said nothing at first, just touched my cheek with her fingertips. Then Dad came up behind her and reached out his big hand to stroke my matted hair. Al, standing at the foot of the bed next to Grandma and Grandpa, gave me an out-and-out grin. I could see the relief in all their faces.

I looked over toward the window—no Aunt Erica. She'd finally flown, probably as soon as Mom got there.

"I'm okay, Mom. I really am," I said, my voice catching.

"You had us so worried," she said.

"I know. I'm sorry."

"Erica should have never taken you down there in the first place!" Mom's eyes clouded with angry tears.

"Where is Aunt Erica?" I asked.

"Waiting outside," Al said. She came around and knelt by the right side of the bed, beside my tractioned leg. "Does it hurt?"

"No. Not really."

"I'm going to sign your cast. I want to be the first one."

"Go right ahead," I told her, smiling.

Mom took hold of my hand. I couldn't stop the tears from springing up. "I love you all," I said, just as the door opened and Aunt Erica came in the room. So she got to hear it, too, and I was glad for that.

"We love you, too," Mom said, before she realized her sister was there.

"Pammy," Aunt Erica said.

Mom stiffened in her chair, then whipped around and shot Aunt Erica an angry, pained look.

"Don't, Mom," I said. "It isn't Aunt Erica's fault. None of this is."

Mom shook her head. "How could you do this?" she yelled at her sister. "How could you endanger my Phoebe?"

"She's okay, Pam." Aunt Erica's voice trembled a bit, but she kept it under control.

"*Okay?*" Mom shrieked. "A broken ankle...all those cuts...hypothermia? You call that *okay?*"

Remaining calm, Aunt Erica said, "I'm sorry, Pam. It's my fault. I knew you'd disapprove of her going and I took her anyway."

"No!" I said emphatically. "It was my choice to go. Aunt Erica didn't make me. None of this is her fault."

Mom shook her head, the muscles of her face all clenched up, as if she couldn't, wouldn't accept it. "*She's* the adult," she said, pointing at Aunt Erica. "*She's* ultimately responsible."

"Mom—" I wriggled my hand out from her grip.

"Everyone…I have to tell you something."

Al's head jerked up, her eyes wide.

I could feel the great weight of it—the lies, the confusion around the lies. We'd all been confused, scrambled, for so long. It was like a fog, making everything seem out of focus.

I took a deep breath. "I know how Bradford died."

Mom was staring at me now. All of them were.

"I saw it. The gun. I wasn't sure at first, but I know now."

"Spider," Grandma said with obvious horror. "Don't—"

"He killed himself," I went on, unable to stop. "He didn't have pneumonia, like you told us." I eyed Al, whose gaze ping-ponged back and forth between Dad and Mom.

"I know why you lied. I know it was to protect us. But lying just made it worse."

A hole had broken in the fog. I could feel it. My mind hurt with the effort of forming these thoughts and speaking them.

Then a surprising thing happened. Grandpa—usually the strong, silent type—broke down. He hadn't cried at the unveiling, but now his hands clenched the footboard, and his body doubled over. He wasn't at all self-conscious. A great wave of grief seemed to flow over him.

As we watched Grandma turn to put her arms around him, I was sure the fog was lifting. It was as if the cries were coming from no one in particular, and from all of us at the same time. They were terrifying. They were a balm.

They were an Amen.

20

We might have all stayed there, just like that, if a nurse hadn't opened the door and poked her head in. "I'm sorry," she said firmly but politely, "but visiting hours are over."

Grandma took Grandpa's arm. "Come on, honey," she coaxed, and helped him toward the door. The sight of my stoic Grandpa, his face pinched with grief, brought more tears to my eyes. Aunt Erica followed them, but Mom, Dad, and Al stayed put.

"We're not leaving," Mom said. "We'll just sit here quietly and let her sleep."

The nurse shook her head. "She needs to rest."

"I'm fine," I told her. "I can sleep with them here, if I need to."

The nurse looked doubtful. "Well, we can give it a try. But only your parents can stay when visiting hours end in twenty minutes." Her eyes fell on Al.

"Okay," Al said.

Then we were alone, the four of us. Mom remained in the bedside chair, Dad behind her.

Al paced the room a few times, then abruptly stopped at the opposite side of the bed and threw up her arms in disgust. "How could you do this to us?" she said to our parents, her voice breaking. "How could you lie?"

"Oh, Al..." Mom began. Her eyes rested on her hands, and she turned her wedding band around and around on her finger. "I was afraid. I didn't want you or Spider to hurt the way I did..." She spoke so softly, my ears strained to catch all her words. "I should have known you were both strong enough. I shouldn't have underestimated you girls."

Al glanced at Mom, then me, with an expression of amazement.

Mom brushed her hair out of her face and stared away from us, through the window. The streetlights looked like artificial stars over the nearly empty lot. "The grief was too much for me already. Knowing how you'd feel if you knew how he'd died—I couldn't cope with that, too." She bowed her head, her hair falling again, a curtain shielding her face. "I am so sorry that I wasn't stronger for you girls. Strong enough to tell the truth."

She looked fragile and alone, as if she'd gone back again in the space of a few moments to the time when she was younger and in such great pain.

I had asked Bradford if Mom would try to take her life again. "I don't know," he'd answered. Once again I felt a chill whooshing through my chest, despite the warm room, the warm blanket.

I would have to live with this, too—this cold, horrible uncertainty. We all would. There were no easy words to make it better.

I covered Mom's hand with my own, and only then did she raise her eyes to mine. "You aren't like me," she said, sounding like Mom again. "I should have known that. I should have seen."

Or Bradford. Or Eli, I thought. But I couldn't say that now, couldn't tell her about reading her diary, or about what I'd seen in the cave. Those words were for another time, or maybe never.

The sight of Bradford and the sound of his voice were still clear in my mind. I wanted to hold them there a while longer. If I let them out into the air now, they might crumble.

Mom's skin felt warm and alive on mine.

The world above ground is just as tricky to navigate as the world below, I thought. Maybe even more so.

"I can stay here with you tonight," Mom said. "That chair is a recliner." She pointed to a lounge chair in the corner.

"No, that's okay," I said.

"Are you sure?" Anxiety flitted across her face.

"I'm sure," I told her.

She hung back, but Dad finally said, "She'll be fine, Pam. All she needs is sleep."

After we all kissed and hugged each other and they were gone, my eyes fell on Al's unfinished writing on my cast.

She'd put it on the front, below the knee, so I

could see it. She had completed only three letters—P-H-O. The beginning of my name.

❧

I didn't wake up until the sun winked at me through the half-shut blinds. The nurse must have come in and lowered them after I fell asleep. I felt groggy and very stiff, and my right leg was numb. It was a huge relief when the physical therapist came in around nine to get me onto crutches. I was no less stiff on my feet, and I had to move very, very slowly—but at least I was moving.

"You'll get the hang of it," said the therapist, a short, muscular man who was probably in his thirties. "In another five or six weeks, you'll be off those crutches."

"Five or six weeks?" I groaned, then sighed. "Guess I won't be doing much running."

He smiled. "Start with walking…around the room."

I did, though being upright made me lightheaded at first, and my leg and all the rest of me dragged heavily. At the far wall, I stopped to look in the mirror above the sink, and drew in a sharp breath to see my face. It was covered with bruises and scrapes, as if I'd been in a prizefight.

"They'll clear up in a couple of days."

I jerked around at the sound of Aunt Erica's voice. She had slipped inside the room so quietly I didn't realize it. She'd cleaned all the dirt off her face and washed her hair, which fell loose around her shoulders. She wore cutoff overalls, a tank top, and sandals. Sunglasses perched at the top of her head.

"You're leaving?"

She nodded. "I've said my good-byes to everyone except you."

I remained motionless, leaning into the sink.

"Well, guess that's enough for now," the physical therapist said, clearing his throat. He led me back to the chair beside my bed. "I'll leave this instruction sheet for you. Take it easy, okay?"

"I'll try," I told him. "Thanks."

As soon as he went out the door, I hobbled over to the window and peered between the blinds slats. It was another hot, bright day, and already sunlight glinted off the cars below.

"We...we stayed up late last night, talking, your mom and I," Aunt Erica said. "Well, more like yelling, at first. She hasn't forgiven me...and I can't really blame her."

I watched her, not reacting visibly, still unsure of myself with her.

"Did you really think it was worth the lie?" I said finally, anger rising in my voice. "Did you think Al and I wouldn't eventually find out anyway?" I lowered myself onto the windowsill.

"No, I didn't. I never thought it was a good idea. I'm telling you, I went along to get along." Aunt Erica bowed her head. "I apologize, Phoebe. I am truly sorry for my part in it." She took a few steps toward me. "You know, Phoebe...it wasn't your mom who asked that we not tell you and Annelise how Bradford died."

"It wasn't?"

"I know you've probably been thinking she did."

"So..." I looked up at the mirror, at my own reflection and hers behind it. Could I trust what she was saying?

"It was your dad," she said.

At first her words didn't register, or maybe I didn't want them to. Then I found myself nodding. It made sense, in a way.

"You know how protective he is of your mom," she said, echoing my thoughts.

"Yeah, but do you think he's sorry? Do you think he knows it was wrong to lie?"

"Give him time. He's probably just feeling over-whelmed like the rest of us. The last few days..." She shot her hand up overhead, like a rocket. *"Wheeee-ooooo,"* she exclaimed, with a feeble smile. "Well, I'd better go. They should be coming to get you soon." She touched my shoulder with her cool hand and leaned over as if to kiss me.

"Wait," I said. "Did Bradford say anything to you before he died? Anything that made you wonder...?"

She shook her head. "No. I hadn't seen him for around a month, and whenever we spoke on the phone, he cut the conversation short. I figured he had a lot of work, or he'd met a girl—" She sighed.

"He had me totally fooled. He didn't sound unhappy. Just...far away."

"Did he leave a note?"

"We looked for one. The police did too. There was nothing."

Suddenly I remembered: He told me he'd left a note in the desk. How had I managed to overlook it?

"I can tell you this," she said softly. "It wasn't completely out of the blue. I knew our cousin Eli, and Bradford was a lot like him. He went up and down so abruptly, and his downs..." she shook her head "...were really down."

Dr. Gloom, telling me to go away—from his door, from the tree roots. Telling me to leave him alone, with his gun...

"I guess he thought that was the only way to find peace," she said, and finally planted a kiss on my forehead.

"Bye," I told her as she crossed the room.

At the door Aunt Erica turned once more, gave me a smile, and then she was gone.

"Are you at peace?" I wondered aloud, imagining Bradford as I'd last seen him, playing with that silver pistol. His face had seemed calm, detached, free of pain.

I squinted against the bars of sunlight, listening to the beating of my heart. "I have a compass," I whispered to him.

Its little arrow was pointing toward home.

21

Soon after Aunt Erica left, Grandma and Grandpa arrived along with Mom, Dad, and Al. Dad filled out my discharge papers so I could leave. Then Grandma and Grandpa said good-bye.

"Phoebe," Grandma said to me quietly, so no one else could hear. She held my cheeks gently in her hands. "Thank you."

"For what?" I said, taken by surprise.

"For your courage." Her hands fell away. "In the cave, and out here. We were wrong..." Her voice broke.

"Grandma, it's okay. Don't worry. I know you're sorry."

"We are," Grandpa said, also speaking low. "Things are going to be different now, I promise you." His eyes darted toward Mom, who, with Dad and Al, was speaking to a nurse at the door.

"What about the house?" I asked.

Grandpa looked at Grandma and brushed away

the tears that had spilled onto her cheeks. "We may try to keep it, if we can," Grandpa said. "We'll be talking about it more with your mom and dad and Erica."

"I hope you can," I said. "I love it."

"I know. Good-bye, sweetheart," Grandma said, and I stood up to kiss her. Grandpa gave me a hug, firmer today, as if he'd figured out that I wouldn't break, that I was strong.

In the car, Mom sat up front with Dad. She dozed on and off while Dad sipped at a super-sized coffee from a gas station market. Al and I were quiet; I guess we slept too. We were all tired. The past year had been an exhausting journey.

At one point, an hour or so into our trip, we were all awake at the same time.

"So how did it happen?" I asked.

Dad's grip on the steering wheel tightened noticeably. Mom turned toward him, her eyes wide.

"Can't it wait?" Al whispered.

Mom turned all the way around and looked at me.

"He wasn't camping with anyone else, was he?" I said.

She shook her head. "He was alone, out in the woods in northern Schoharie County." She recited the facts quietly. "Some hikers found him later that day. One stayed with him while the others went for help."

"He wasn't dead?" I said, terrified at the thought

that Bradford could have waited there for hours, slowly losing life.

"Oh, yes, he was," Mom said. "That was instantaneous. They needed help to...to bring him out of there."

Al sat forward, her arms clenched across her stomach. "Please," she said. "I'm feeling really sick."

Mom reached across the seat back and touched her forehead. "Sorry, honey."

"And you had no ceremony for him, none at all," I said. "No funeral, no mourning..."

"Girls," Dad said. "Let's take a break for now, okay? We can talk about this when we get home."

I could see his weary smile in the rearview mirror. The skin around his eyes looked as fragile as parchment.

I felt the question on my lips. "Why?" Al leaned forward, too, as if she were going to question him. I pulled her back.

"Shhh," I whispered. "Let him drive."

She started to protest, then fell back. Later, I would tell her what Aunt Erica told me. How Dad started the lie. But right now, I just squeezed her arm.

Dad turned on the radio and scanned stations up and down the dial for nearly the entire rest of the way home.

❧

Our street didn't look quite the same. I had been away for just a couple of days, so why did the trees seem so much greener? Why did the houses look so much prettier, so much more distinct?

As soon as we got inside the house, Dad opened up the convertible couch in the living room. I thought maybe he would lie down on it himself and nap, he looked so exhausted; but of course, it was for me. Gratefully I took it, propping my knee up with pillows the way the physical therapist had instructed.

I slept until late afternoon. When I woke up, I saw Mom at the end of the bed, sketching on a memo pad, her motions quick and delicate. She hadn't yet realized I was awake. There was something different in her face—if not peace, then at least understanding.

"Hi, sleepyhead," she said, smiling, when she finally saw me looking at her. "Dinner will be ready soon."

I'd been dreaming of the cave—of the amber formation, the glow stone. It was even more beautiful than I'd remembered, and as I looked at it, its colors and textures began to change, to reconfigure, until a piece of it dropped off into my hand. And then it was gone, just as if it had dissolved into my skin.

"Mom," I said. "I saw Bradford in the cave."

She winced, but she didn't move away.

I tried to sit up, and Mom, seeing me struggle, placed some couch cushions behind my back and head.

"I spoke to him, Mom. He looked so real, so much like himself..." My throat grew suddenly dry, scratchy. I knew if I cried now, I couldn't finish. "He showed me the way out of the cave."

"Oh, Spider—" She inhaled sharply.

"I know it sounds crazy. But it was...it seemed...so real."

"No," she said, "I believe you. I think that help comes to us at extreme times. Whether he was a hallucination or not doesn't matter—" She gently stroked my hair. "Once," she said, "someone came back to help me...but I was too frightened to listen."

My mouth opened. Much as I wanted to, I couldn't bring myself to speak.

"I think you know that, don't you, honey? When I noticed that my diary was gone, I figured you had taken it. I found it under your mattress."

Her voice was even, not at all accusatory. Still, I felt myself blushing fiercely.

"I was going to pack it away, with some other books and things I didn't need anymore—or didn't think I needed." A smile flickered across her face. "I was wrong about that, like about so much else."

"I really didn't know what it was," I told her. "It just looked like an old, pretty book, and I wondered why you had put it in that great big pile. And then I opened it—"

"And you read about Eli...the mirror...what happened after?"

I nodded slowly, my ears buzzing with shame. "Mom, I'm so sorry I took it."

Her fingertips again brushed my hair. "That's okay. I was upset at first, I admit…but once we heard what happened to you in the cave…" Her eyes darkened. "I realized I was wrong to think you were like me…"

She went on, her tone changed, fear and admiration now mixed in her voice. "You know, I never would have gone in that cave in the first place. I wouldn't have had the courage."

"Mom," I said, "it was fantastic. Even the hard parts."

She got up, took the two photos from the mantle, and brought them back to the sofa bed. We sat there looking at them, side by side.

"They looked so much alike," she said, lightly touching the glass over Eli's face, then Bradford's.

"There were alike, weren't they?"

"In some ways," she murmured, then turned to me. "It always struck me, though, how much like Brad *you* were. Your interest in science, rocks…and a certain fearlessness." She held her palms over her eyes momentarily, as if remembering. "I was a lot like Eli. More of a dreamer. He painted, too, you know."

"He did?

She nodded. "He could have been very good."

I felt a wrenching in my chest. So much was lost.

Then Bradford's words came back to me. "Nothing was lost." But he wasn't talking about himself, or Eli. He was talking about my satchel— and maybe, about me.

"Mom," I said, "I'm keeping the desk."

"I know," she whispered.

We cried then, a good, fog-dispelling soaker, and by the end we had our arms around each other. Afterward, we pulled back and sat quietly for a time.

"What did you sketch?" I asked after a while.

She turned her pad toward me. It showed the sofa bed with a sail, riggings, and me on it, holding a spyglass up to my eye.

"Remember how you girls used to pretend our bed was a sailing ship?"

I nodded, smiling. "Saturday mornings, before cartoons."

She sighed. "We've been through some pretty choppy waters."

"But look. We haven't capsized. The pirates haven't gotten us. We're still afloat."

We sat without talking, in the peace that follows the storm, her hands resting on mine.

22

May, 2005

I hold the burning match to the wick and wait a moment until it catches, the tiny yellow flame lengthening upward as Mom recites the Hebrew prayer. When she is done I say my own.

"This is for you, Bradford. I wish I could have known you longer. I wish your compass had pointed you toward life."

"We love you," Al adds.

I picture him as he'd been in life, as he was in the cave. The flame seems a meager memorial to someone so smart, to someone more friend than uncle. At the same time, it is a fitting symbol of his bright, flickering spirit.

Then, as we linger before the flame, I think of his note, about how much I wanted to look for it during that first week after the cave. When my ankle had finally healed enough to manage the stairs, I went down to the old garage. After searching awhile I found the note wedged in the crack between the bottom and side of the crystal drawer. It still spooks me to think that if I hadn't seen Uncle Bradford in the cave, I might never have discovered it.

Mom takes a pitcher of iced tea out of the refrigerator and we sit down together at the table. I know we won't have many more times like this, and I can tell Mom and Dad are aware of it, too. They keep looking at each other, at Al and me, as if to imprint a snapshot in their minds.

In a few months, Al will be off at college in New York. In a few weeks, we'll both be starting summer jobs as counselors, she at an art camp, and I at a summer science program for kids.

"Tell us one more time," Mom says, "about the cave."

I take a deep breath. The memories are still so close that I can see them in my mind and feel them on my skin. The descent through the gopher hole. The Pictograph Crawl. Hearing the voice and following it. Falling in the stream. Bradford reaching down to me and pulling me out. Finding my way to the sunlit chamber...

"He asked me to forgive him," I finally say.

"Have you?" Mom asks.

I nod. "I think so."

Dad coughs, his eyes fixed on the flame. "That is something I've had trouble doing," he says awkwardly, his face flushing. "I blamed him not only for hurting himself, but for hurting all of us." He shakes his glass gently, clinking the ice cubes. "But I can see things more clearly now. I know he couldn't help himself."

We all look up at him, and his eyes flicker nervously between my sister and me. I glance at Al, who nods in understanding. It's as if we are sharing a thought at that moment: Dad isn't talking just about Bradford, but himself.

I reach my arm around him and give him a hug.

Mom says nothing more. She rises and leaves the room, a signal that our ceremony is over. Later, though, in the twilight, I see her in her bedroom, painting. She started again last winter, taking all her paints and brushes and canvasses down from the attic. Dad even put her art back on the stairwell wall, and she didn't argue.

On her canvas is the beginning of a face, ghostly, as if a reflection. It could be Eli, or Brad, or herself. Or someone else entirely. The details aren't put in yet, except for the eyes, mottled with streaks and spots like matching stones staring out of the canvas—eerily lifelike, intense, questioning.

METAMORPHIC

The doorknob turns easily, and I open the red door. My feet feel their way down the three short steps. Then my right hand reaches out and touches wood. I open the drawer I usually visit first. On top of the crystal specimens sits a small, folded piece of paper, buttery smooth from being handled so much.

> Dear Phoebe,
>   Hard and soft,
>   fixed and molten.
>   Find the way
>   between the extremes.
>   Never settle.
>   Never set.
>   Always see the gems
>   in dark places.
>   Love,
>   Bradford

My throat tightens, as it always does. I refold the paper and place it back in the drawer. I will take the note when I leave this house, along with a few pieces: obsidian, to remind me of the darkness down below; a chunk of biotite gneiss, for what I left behind; and the glow stone, which I carry in my heart.

The rest will wait for me.

A dream inspired the story of THE GLOW STONE. "I saw the figure of a girl," Ellen Dreyer says, "huddled, alone, inside a cave." After making several journeys underground, the author

found that the experience of caving is not unlike the process of writing a book. "You have to go deep inside yourself, often feeling around in the dark, to find out what it is you want to say."

Ellen is a freelance editor and the author of numerous chapter books for young readers. She also teaches creative writing to middle and high school students. She lives in Maplewood, New Jersey. THE GLOW STONE is her first novel for young adults.

For more information about Ellen Dreyer, please visit her website at *ellendreyer.com*.